"You're Shari! Why?

Griff's question made Shari blush deeply. She couldn't look into his eyes, only managed to whisper, "Please, Griff, just let me pass."

But Griff reached out and gently grasped a handful of her dark lustrous hair, and Shari, without really knowing why, knew she had wanted him to restrain her.

"When I first bought Jet she was a skittish, nervous foal, too wild to handle. But I'm a patient man; I tamed her." And then he added softly, "You remind me of her."

Shari, mesmerized by his hold on her, could only stare at him speechlessly. Her senses now were totally awakened by his touch.

"Are you too wild to hold, Shari? Somehow, in spite of your don't-touch-me manner I think I'll tame you, too!"

Annabel Murray has pursued many hobbies. She helped found an arts group in Liverpool, England, where she lives with her husband and two daughters. She loves drama: she appeared in many stage productions and went on to write an award-winning historical play. She uses all her experiences—holidays being no exception—to flesh out her character's backgrounds and create believable settings for her romance novels.

Books by Annabel Murray

These books may be available at your local bookseller.

Don't miss any of our special offers. Write to us at the following address for information on our newest releases.

Harlequin Reader Service
901 Fuhrmann Blvd., P.O. Box 1397, Buffalo, NY 14240
Canadian address: P.O. Box 603,
Fort Erie, Ont. L2A 5X3

Wild for to Hold

Annabel Murray

Harlequin Books

TORONTO • NEW YORK • LONDON
AMSTERDAM • PARIS • SYDNEY • HAMBURG
STOCKHOLM • ATHENS • TOKYO • MILAN

Original hardcover edition published in 1986
by Mills & Boon Limited

ISBN 0-373-02819-9

Harlequin Romance first edition February 1987

For Tom, my husband,
who wanted me to write another book
about the lakes

There is written her fair neck round about
Noli me tangere, for Caesar's I am
And wild for to hold, though I seem tame.
(Sir Thomas Wyatt)

CHAPTER ONE

'JIMMY! You can't mean it! Tell me it isn't true!' Her large, violet eyes full of dismay, Shari Freeman came to a halt on the steep fellside and looked up at her tall companion. She shivered miserably in the damp March morning mist, which, until now, had not troubled her.

'It's hardly the kind of thing I'd joke about!' Jimmy Crosthwaite's amiable, nice-looking face wore a rueful expression. 'I thought perhaps I'd better tell you ... give you a chance to get used to the idea before your grandmother mentions it herself.' Jimmy was, Shari could tell, equally upset by the news he'd had to impart. Twenty-six, four years older than her, Jimmy had always been the recipient of her confidences, pleasant or otherwise; and he had been a tower of strength in the last few unhappy weeks.

'I just can't believe it!' A shake of the glossy, shoulder-length, black hair expressed Shari's uhappy bewilderment. Her full soft mouth quivered a little. 'Poor, darling Gran ... she's lived at Threlkeld all her married life. How could she bear to sell up? Does she really need to?'

'It *is* necessary, Shari! Believe me! ... and it's practically decided as far as I can make out. The buyer hasn't actually seen the farm and the house yet, but ... Look, Shar' ... you won't make a fuss about it? ... I mean ...'

'Of course I shan't make a scene!' Shari's grave, oval face flushed indignantly. 'I'm surprised you think I would, especially since Gran's so poorly.'

'You wouldn't *mean* to,' Jimmy said hastily, 'of course I know that. You'd try reasoning with her,

7

though . . . pleading with her. But there's no point. She can't afford to change her mind and you do have a tendency to go off like a firecracker when you don't agree with something, and where Threlkeld's concerned.' He shrugged expressively.

Shari remained silent. She couldn't deny the truth of his remark; and it was never any good anyway getting annoyed with Jimmy, the attraction of whose company lay in his sweet good nature, which would not permit him to quarrel with her. Her grandmother was not at present up to coping with discussions and arguments. Following the recent death of her son, Shari's father, Abigail Freeman had suffered a series of minor strokes and it was the concern of everyone around her to spare her the slightest stress.

'How come you seem to know so much?'

'Your grandmother told mine, and Gran thought *she* ought to tell *me*. After all, it might make a difference to my job.'

It followed, Sari mused. Old Lily Crosthwaite had been housekeeper and general factotum at Threlkeld Hall since Abigail Freeman had come there as a bride, nervous of her new dignity as a rich farmer's wife. Unused to servants, she had made a friend of Lily; their children had grown up side by side, and now their grandchildren.

'Try not to worry about it for the moment,' Jimmy said, looking anxiously at Shari's drawn face. 'I wish I hadn't told you till later. Come on, cheer up! It's the first trail of the season and Spectre's going to win, aren't you boy?' He looked down at the hound that trotted quietly at his heels.

Together they'd been training Spectre since he was an eight-month-old puppy, urging him to follow a short trail around a field, left by the aroma of an old stocking, dipped in aniseed and paraffin. Today was his first big race and both Shari and Jimmy were hoping that he was ready to chase the sharp scent for ten miles, across some of the most mountainous country in England.

'I hope he'll do well, but he is only a novice, Jimmy,' Shari reminded him, momentarily diverted from their unhappy topic of conversation, but then, returning to it, 'Do you know who the buyer is?'

'Yes, that's something else I ought to warn you about. The person who's interested in buying Threlkeld is some kind of distant relation to old Charlie Garner. Comes from down south somewhere, and Charlie's bound to be at the trail today. Better not say anything disparaging about the sale, or the buyer, in front of Charlie.'

'A relation of Charlie's?' Intensely loyal to her friends, Shari expected the same kind of consideration from them. Charlie Garner was an old family friend, an honorary uncle, who'd taught her to ride her first pony, taught her fell and mountain craft, so that now she was as agile as a goat or sheep upon the Lakeland crags, their every aspect and mood well known to her. 'Charlie's a friend of ours. I can't believe he'd encourage an "off-comer", relation or not, to buy property in the Beckdale Valley.'

'Oh, come on, Shari love. I know you've had good reason for your distrust of outsiders, what with your Mum going off the way she did, and then Mary Cranford belittling Threlkeld. But that was all a long time ago and it's time you got over your prejudice. Not everyone's like that. Besides,' Jimmy pointed out reasonably, 'I think Mr Garner thought he was acting *as* a friend. He knew your grandmother wanted . . . well . . . no . . . *had* to sell up, and mentioned it to this relation of his. Apparently he's prepared to offer a very good price, probably more than anyone else, because Threlkeld is just what he's looking for; and if he's a relation of Charlie's, he can't be that bad.'

'My mother was one of *my* relations,' Shari said bitterly, 'so that argument doesn't follow, and anyway Threlkeld is our home, Gran's and mine. It's the only one I've ever known.' There was despair as well as anger in the words. 'Where do we go? Suppose the upheaval kills Gran? Old people can't do with being uprooted, and she's still far from well.'

'I don't know any more than I've told you,' Jimmy said patiently, 'and I'm beginning to wish I hadn't said *anything*. But I thought you'd be sensible, you usually are about most things. Come on, brace up, there's a good girl. At least try and *look* cheerful. We're there.'

It was still misty at the top of the Bendfell pass. Grey, boiling clouds swirling over the close, sheep-cropped turf, obscured the outlines of the dry-stone walls. Here a group of twenty men or so, cloth-capped and breeched, had gathered, each with a hound on a short lead. Shari watched as Jimmy joined them, knowing that for the moment she was forgotten. Men and hounds formed a line, removed their animals' leads and waited for the signal to start. There it was, a sharp whistle and with a concerted chorus of yelps, the hounds were off, streaks of darker colour against the swirling whiteness of the mist.

As Jimmy, with the other men, waited anxiously for the reappearance of his dog. Shari sat on a nearby, lichen-encrusted boulder and considered the unpleasant news she had just received.

She had been born and raised in the large, rambling farmhouse in the Beckdale Valley; going no further afield than Kendal for her schooling, asking for nothing better afterwards than to return to Threlkeld, to work alongside her father on the fell and mountain land belonging to her widowed grandmother, and this she had done for the last four years. True, at the time, Abigail Freeman had suggested diffidently that it was no life for an eighteen-year-old, would even have liked

Shari to go abroad, to a finishing school, to learn the ladylike ways she considered her granddaughter lacked. But the necessary finances had not been available and besides, the thought had filled the tom-boyish Shari with horror. She was grateful that her father had laughed off his mother's suggestion, content to have Shari as a substitute for the son his wife had never given him.

Shari had never felt that she 'fitted in' with the other girls at her exclusive school, but, on one particular holiday, almost in the nature of an experiment, she had brought a friend home to Beckdale: Mary Cranford, a student in her own year at the sixth-form college and who, herself a farmer's daughter, might be expected to have something in common with Shari. Before the visit, she had described Threlkeld in the glowing terms of her own love for it. But to Mary Cranford the Beckdale Valley was isolated, relatively small, only suited really to sheep farming, with little chance of expansion. Mary had been unable to hide her boredom with the quiet life the valley afforded and on the flimsiest of excuses had cut short her stay. Shari, sensitive to the reaction of others to her home, had been mortified. Almost she dreaded meeting Mary again, wondering if the other girl would hold Beckdale up to ridicule before the rest of their classmates.

But Shari was a fighter; and despite her unhappiness at school she had completed her final term, obtained her A-levels; but then she had returned to the Beckdale Valley, determined never to leave it again for any length of time and with a distaste for outsiders almost as strong as her father's. Jack Freeman had been an embittered man for some years. Elizabeth Freeman, Shari's mother, had been what the dalesfolk called an 'off-comer'. City bred, she had never managed to fit into her husband's life at Threlkeld and finally, when her daughter was ten, Elizabeth had walked out to 'return to civilisation'; and Shari had been left in the care of Lily Crosthwaite, the housekeeper, looking upon Lily's orphaned grandson, Jimmy, as the brother she'd never had.

Shari had soon fallen back into the gentle, familiar ways of farm life, gladly putting her schooldays behind her. Happily, diligently, she had worked as hard as any of the men, never dreaming that this pattern of life could ever change so drastically. But it had, just three months ago, with her father's death. Hauling logs with a tractor on a precipitous fellside, Jack Freeman had, uncharacteristically, underestimated the slope and the tractor had toppled, rolling over and crushing him beneath it.

For the past few months work had gone on as usual in the hands of a few loyal farmworkers. But Abigail Freeman was old and frail, Shari hadn't a man's physical strength for the heavier work, and now, Jimmy told her, their finances were in a bad way.

Shari had to admit that to sell up was the obvious solution, but surely it wasn't the only one? Couldn't they obtain a loan? she wondered. She still felt that, with help, she was capable of maintaining Threlkeld, which she had hoped would some day be her inheritance. But if Jimmy were to be believed about their financial straits, not all Shari's experience, her willingness to work alongside the men, could alter things. Then too the farm *was* Abigail's and she had the right to sell up, and it would be far more painful for her grandmother, after fifty years, to leave the house which had been the scene of her happy married life, than for Shari, who had all her life still before her.

She would just have to put aside her own selfish considerations. After the sale she would try and find some kind of job, though what exactly she would do was a mystery as yet. Her only experience was in farming and for the first time in her life, she found herself regretting that she hadn't yielded to Abigail's persuasion and acquired other skills. The job would have to be connected with animals in some way. Perhaps someone would take her on as a stable lad? She was good with horses.

It was a pity this crisis couldn't have been delayed until the somewhat hazy future, when she might have been married, with a husband capable of taking charge. She probably would marry some day, she mused vaguely. But at the moment it was not something to consider seriously. She'd never been in love and because of her relatively secluded life, she had never even met a man who stirred in her the kind of feelings she imagined love brought in its wake.

Perhaps she *wouldn't* get married. Her grandmother, in one of her rare moments of tartness, had commented that most men liked their women to be feminine, not hoydenish creatures in shabby, boyish clothes, and Shari had never been one for dressing up. She had never been more delighted than on the day when she had forever abandoned her school uniform and reverted to her beloved, well-worn jeans and shirts.

A sudden roar of excited voices interrupted her thoughts, telling her that the hounds had been sighted, and she ran to Jimmy's side, straining her eyes to identify Spectre. There was a wild mêlée of muzzles, legs, lashing tails and panting tongues, as, hearts thumping, coats glistening with moisture, the dogs rejoined their owners.

'Third!' Jimmy said, trying vainly to keep the disappointment out of his voice. 'Not bad for a young'un.'

'In point of fact you've got a good dog there, lad, one to be reckoned with, when he's had a bit more experience.' The speaker was a solid, chunkily built man of medium height, his face as rugged as the countryside he inhabited, his countenance enlivened by bright blue eyes, an old fashioned moustache and a stiff brush of white hair. 'Hallo, Shari!' The blue eyes twinkled affectionately.

'Good morning, Charlie!' Shari said formally, her manner a little stiff. Despite her resolution to face up to things and not make the wrench even harder for her grandmother, she couldn't help it. A relation of his might soon be living in *her* home.

Disconsolately she turned away, drifting back down the fellside, slender shoulders hunched, hands thrust into the pockets of her faded jeans. The early morning mist had cleared now and the day was coldly, crisply blue, so that all Beckdale lay spread out below her, like a richly patterned carpet, the incredibly complex crisscross of stone walls on green fields, the pale sunshine shining on the weathered grey of the village with its tiny inn, farm workers' cottages and a small church; and, set apart from all this, Threlkeld Hall and its outbuildings. Steep fells and jagged mountain ridges embraced the little valley, which, with its own tiny lake, was effectively cut off from the rest of civilisation.

Lying between the Borrowdale and Langdale Fells and south of Glencora, Beckdale was very difficult of access, served only by a twisting narrow road from Pebblethwaite. The nearest of the larger lakes, Wastwater and Thirlmere, were ten miles distant in either direction and could only be reached after negotiating some tricky terrain. It was not, Shari often gave thanks, motoring country, but the perfect area for walking and riding and as yet totally unspoilt by tourist encroachment.

Jimmy and Spectre caught her up at a run.

'Bit short with poor old Charlie, weren't you?' Jimmy never scolded, but, in a reasonable manner, he had a habit of pointing out her faults and, irritatingly, he was always right.

'I couldn't help it,' she retorted. 'Charlie of all people! Encouraging one of his relations to buy my roof from over my head!'

'Actually,' Jimmy pointed out, with more truth than tact, 'it isn't your roof. It's Mrs Freeman's, and it's *got to be sold*!'

'But if we hadn't got to sell up, it would have been mine some day, surely? If Dad hadn't died, she'd have left it to him; and eventually he'd have left it to me.'

'Not necessarily. Even if your father had still been alive, you'd soon have had to face the fact that the farm isn't paying its way, hasn't been for a long time.'

Shari accepted that Jimmy probably knew more than she did about the financial state of Threlkeld. He ran the farm office and did the accounts.

'If the place *is* in such a poor way, why does this . . . this *person* . . . want to buy it?'

'Perhaps he's rich,' the ever-practical Jimmy suggested, 'perhaps he can afford to make improvements, more stock, more up-to-date farming methods.'

'Changes at Threlkeld? Horrible thought.' Shari shuddered. Then another thought occurred to her, causing her again to put aside her personal feelings.

'Do you think the new man will keep everyone on? The farmhands? The old shepherd? You?'

'No idea,' Jimmy said soberly, 'wish I had. I don't want to leave Threlkeld any more than you do. In a kind of way, it's my home too.'

'Oh!' she cried, her violet eyes filling with tears which she despised, but could not help. 'Why did things have to change? Why did Dad have to have that accident? Why couldn't everything have gone on as it always did?'

Tentatively, Jimmy put an arm about her shoulders. Tomboyish, her only sentimentality that for her home, she shunned displays of emotion or affection. But today she accepted the caress.

'Don't worry, Shari, maybe things will work out better than you think. Try and put a good face on it for your Gran's sake.'

She pulled away, dashing an impatient hand across her eyes, ashamed of her momentary weakness. She never cried. Clutching at the small hope he offered, she said:

'Yes, of course, perhaps you're right. I must think of Gran. Do you think if I got a job it would help?'

'I think it might be a good idea if you *thought* of getting a job, but, no, it wouldn't do away with the necessity for selling up.'

'Oh well,' she said despondently, 'let's go home. Your Gran will be dying to know how Spectre got on; and I'll try not to moan, honestly I will, about Threlkeld.'

Jimmy sighed as he followed her. He studied her slight, boyish figure as she strode ahead of him. He was very fond of Shari, but for all her twenty-two years she was still very young, still tomboyish, almost unfeminine in her ways. They had been friends a long time and he knew her perhaps better than she knew herself. It might be a good thing that Shari was going to be forced to leave the valley, to see new places, make new friends, perhaps meet some man who would appreciate her sterling worth, teach her that there was more to life than working alongside farmhands being treated with an easy camaraderie, as if she were in fact a boy. She needed to realise that there was more to life than striding over her beloved fells, or galloping her spunky pony. He sighed again. Poor Shari! Despite her brave words, he knew she wouldn't be able to hide her feelings. She had an awful lot to learn and he had a feeling that the process wouldn't be without hurt.

They continued their descent of the fellside, coming at last to the floor of the Beckdale Valley, following its narrow length through the village and beyond to the farm. The first sight of Threlkeld Hall, no matter how short the time she had been away from it, always brought a curious, tight feeling to Shari's throat. She loved it so much, every one of its solid, reassuring, grey stones, glinting in the sunlight like dull silver, stones primrose-hued with lichens. But today affection went deeper, threatening to choke her, nausea churning her stomach at the thought of losing all this. It was a beautiful old place, neither just a farmhouse nor quite a manor house, a typical, grey-stone, Lakeland building, with thick walls and heavy slate roof. Standing foursquare in its own quiet acres among trees and backed by rounded green hills, it defied the elements.

Behind the house, rough sheep tracks and grassy loanings climbed the fell and beyond were the mountains, craggy and grim at times, yet strangely beautiful too, gorse-clad in summer, mist-shrouded in autumn, shining, white-capped under winter snow. To one side, a huge, stone archway framed big wooden doors, which opened into a courtyard, along one side of which were stables; and on the other side, the house adjoined an enormous barn.

Shari and Jimmy entered the house via the back door, which opened into a warm, spacious and friendly kitchen, the air at this time of day fragrant with cooking smells.

'Gran! We're back!' Jimmy announced unnecessarily, since old Lily Crosthwaite's crab-apple face was already turned eagerly in his direction. 'Spectre came third.'

'Well enough for a first attempt!' The old woman gave the hound a tit-bit, then, to Shari, 'You'll be wanted in the drawing-room, lass. Mrs Freeman's got visitors.' Though lifelong friends, since their early twenties, Lily had never referred to Abigail other than in this formal manner.

'Visitors? What sort of visitors?' Shari stiffened apprehensively.

'Folk, happen, that mean to buy Threlkeld. I suppose our Jimmy's told you by now?' Her bright brown gaze darted from Shari to her grandson and he nodded

'Just as well I did, apparently. I didn't know they were expected so soon.'

'You'd best change, Miss Shari,' Lily continued. 'You can't appear in your grandma's drawing-room in that mucky outfit.'

Shari looked down the length of her own slim figure. Jeans and sweater had seen better days and the morning's encounter with the damp fellside had not improved their appearance, but still ... She lifted her chin, her whole face assuming stubborn lines.

'It's Threlkeld they've come to look over, not me! They'll have to put up with me as I am.'

The stone-floored kitchen was linked by a long corridor to the drawing-room and Shari dawdled, unwilling to encounter the strangers. Once she had done so, their presence would become an unpleasant reality. Of all the rooms in the house, after the kitchen she loved the drawing-room best, especially in winter and the cold, early months of spring. Its low-beamed, white-walled, chintzy décor was dominated by a great fireplace, which in one evening could consume a wheelbarrow full of logs. To open the door to the room was to be enveloped in the cosy glow of this log fire.

Certainly its warm appeal seemed to be appreciated by the couple who sat before it, looking at Abigail Freeman in her deep, cushioned armchair. Shari's hostile gaze was drawn first to the woman. She was not of a type often seen in this part of the country, tall, endowed with a figure of generous but shapely proportions; her magnolia-pale skin was framed by wave after wave of deep, mahogany-red hair, that reflected the flames flickering behind her. There her beauty ended, Shari considered; her eyes seemed hard and shrewd, the vividly outlined mouth determined-looking. The room was cloyed by a heavy, musky perfume, which could only emanate from the visitor. Abigail Freeman favoured light, floral colognes.

'Ah, Shari! There you are! Miss Garner, Mr Masterson, *this* is my granddaughter.' The last words were said with affectionate pride, but the reproachful expression in Abigail's eyes told Shari that she should have heeded Lily's advice and changed before appearing in the drawing-room.

The woman made no move apart from a nod and a brief smile; and for her own part, Shari just could not bring herself to offer to shake hands with the interlopers. The man, however, rose and crossed the room in a few, long, easy strides, holding out his hand and Shari took critical stock of him, the 'off-comer', the usurper.

He was very tall, was her immediate thought. She couldn't recall ever encountering so tall a man. He must be six foot two at least. Blunt features, not handsome but attractively ugly, were composed of a broad, slightly crooked nose, large, well shaped mouth and very vivid, sapphire-blue eyes.

'Hallo, Shari, Griff Masterson. I'm glad to meet you at last. We've been hearing a great deal about you.' His voice was a deep, gravelly, but educated drawl. The eyes meeting hers were steady, their expression honest, open.

Reluctantly, she allowed her slender hand to rest in his, intending to withdraw it immediately, but it was enclosed by strong, hard fingers, warm and unexpectedly pleasing to the touch. So many men she'd encountered outside the valley had limp, unpleasant handshakes, rather like encountering the damp, lolling tongue of a cow. But she didn't want to approve of anything about this man and she withdrew her hand abruptly, stepping back from him, her grave little face unsmiling, unfriendly.

'I suppose *you're* the one who wants to buy Threlkeld Hall?' she challenged, her normally husky, melodic voice ringing unusually high with the chagrin she could not hide.

He laughed, the extension of his wide mouth revealing large, very white teeth, perfect, except for the gap at the front, which only seemed to increase the humorous appeal of his smile.

'Not guilty! I'm not the villain of the piece, as you obviously regard *any* prospective purchaser. The *villainess* is Estelle, Miss Garner.' He indicated the red-haired woman, who looked a little irritated by the epithet he had applied to her, but inclined her head again.

Garner? Of course! The same name as Charlie's! Why hadn't she realised when her grandmother had introduced the couple? It had never crossed her mind that the prospective buyer might be female, and certainly not a woman like this! She'd be a complete misfit in Beckdale ... like my mother, came the thought.

'*You're* related to Charlie Garner?' she said incredulously. This smooth, svelte, feline-looking creature bore no resemblance to the blunt, stocky dales-man.

'Charles Garner is my uncle by marriage.' The reply, though brief, was spoken in a clear, pleasant voice.

'I thought he wouldn't be a blood relative!' Shari said, unaware that her obvious satisfaction could be regarded as insulting.

'Shari!' her grandmother said sharply, but Griff Masterson interposed, deflecting the reproach.

'Since Estelle's stepfather is Charlie's brother, I suppose they can't be expected to have the same blood. However,' he gave one of his brilliant smiles to the other woman, 'I agree with you that Estelle is certainly better looking.'

The air of tension created by Shari's blunt remark was eased. Shari heard her grandmother's relieved sigh, saw Estelle's little smile of amusement. But meeting Griff Masterson's blue eyes, she knew that he at least shared her own knowledge that her remark had *not* been intended as a compliment to Estelle.

'I suppose Jimmy told Shari that I'm thinking of selling Threlkeld,' Abigail Freeman said. Her voice was regretful. 'I don't *want* to, goodness knows, yet it's the only practical solution to our difficulties.' She shook her grey head. 'But I don't know what my late husband would have thought of the changes you have in mind.'

'What changes?' Shari demanded sharply.

'I don't think Mrs Freeman's grandchild need concern herself with that, do you, darling?' Estelle laid a red-tipped hand on Griff's arm as he seemed about to answer the question. Her hazel eyes regarded Shari's youthful and untidy appearance with amusement. 'She's bound to disapprove. The young are so hot-headed.'

'Child! The young!' Shari's violet eyes could appear black when she was angered. 'For your information, I'm *not* a child.' She drew herself up to her full five feet three. 'I'll be twenty-three in two months' time.'

Griff Masterson shook his blond head in mock despair.

'Incredibly ancient!' he said, straight-faced, but with a trace of laughter in eyes and mouth. 'In that case, I don't feel we *would* be justified in hiding the awful truth from you.' Griff it seemed had a wry sense of humour, which, unwillingly, Shari found appealed to her.

Estelle, however, was impatient to return to business.

'Griff, don't tease the ... don't tease Miss Freeman. Surely what we do with the property when we move in is nobody's business but ours?'

Shari could see the look of trouble deepening on Abigail Freeman's face and she knew it was up to her to cut short a discussion which promised to become distressing to her grandmother.

'Don't worry!' she said shortly. 'I couldn't care less *what* you do, so long as I'm not around to see it.

Gran!' She placed a hand on her grandmother's shoulder. 'Do you need me any more? I didn't have a chance to muck out Rainbow's stall this morning, Jimmy and I were out so early.'

'Well, dear,' her grandmother's face had cleared a little, but not altogether, 'I *was* hoping that whilst Miss Garner and I talk over financial matters, you would show Mr Masterson around. He hasn't been here before and . . .'

Shari hesitated, then,

'Oh, all right!' she said grudgingly.

'Perhaps I could be of some help to you?' Griff enquired pleasantly, as he followed her through a side door and into the stable yard.

Shari cast a downward glance at his sharply creased trousers and highly polished brogues and her small nose curled disdainfully.

'Dressed like *that*?' she enquired. 'Besides,' she couldn't resist the taunt, 'you might get your hands dirty!' She didn't imagine the highly perfumed Estelle would relish getting her boyfriend back reeking of the farmyard. Yet he didn't *look* the lounge-lizard type. His face was deeply tanned, as though he were accustomed to spending much time out of doors, and the appearance of his fair hair reinforced that evidence, being bleached as though from exposure to strong sunlight.

'My hands are quite accustomed to hard work,' he replied calmly, holding them out for her inspection. They were indeed not the hands of the idle dilettante she had expected them to be, but broad, strong and capable, with slightly spatulate fingers; his palms bore calluses and scars which had not been lightly obtained. They were rather nice hands in fact. 'And I'm sure one of your farm-hands could lend me some wellingtons.'

'Why are you so keen to muck out my horse's stable?' she asked suspiciously. 'You don't have to curry favour with *me*, you know. *I* have no say in whether or not Gran sells Threlkeld to your girlfriend. I wish I *did*!' she concluded bitterly.

He seemed unperturbed by her question and her hostile manner.

'I assure you my motives are purely selfish, a need to get my hand in again for future use, since it seems in Estelle's mind at least, the purchase is a foregone conclusion.'

'Get your hand in? At mucking out horses? Why should *you* need to do that? And what's that got to do with Miss Garner buying Threlkeld? We have no horses, except my mare, Rainbow, and the Shire.'

'I seem to remember,' and again there was that suspicion of laughter in his voice, 'that you didn't care to know Estelle's plans, didn't want to see them put into operation, so I must decline to answer. I couldn't possibly be responsible for disturbing your peace of mind.'

Hateful, sarcastic pig! This time Shari missed the humour and was relieved instead that she could find something about Griff Masterson to dislike. So far he had compared very favourably with Estelle and she was determined to dislike both of them equally.

'Anyhow, I'd rather Jimmy and I mucked Rainbow out,' she stated flatly, 'she doesn't care for strangers, *any more than we do*!'

' "We" including Jimmy, I presume? Exactly who is Jimmy?'

'My friend,' she said shortly, 'my very best friend, who's probably going to lose his home and his job when your Miss Garner takes over.'

'Ah, your boyfriend. I begin to understand. Not only are we breaking up the happy home, but there's a risk of blighting your romance.'

'No, I ...' she began, then stopped. Some faint, intuitive sense told her that it might be politic to confirm his belief. 'Nobody could split me and Jimmy up.' It was true. They had always been as close as brother and sister.

'I see!' Sapphire-blue eyes regarded her thoughtfully, but he made no further comment. Instead he changed the subject.

'And what about you? What will you do when Threlkeld is sold?'

'Find a job, I suppose, preferably something to do with animals. But Threlkeld *isn't* sold yet; and I'd rather somebody local bought it, someone who loves the area as much as we do.'

'Hmm! Oh, well, since I'm not allowed to make myself useful, you may as well show me round. How far does the property actually extend, in terms of land?'

She told him, then, bluntly, she asked,

'Just what is *your* interest, Mr Masterson? Since it's Miss Garner who'll be buying Threlkeld, or thinks she will!'

He regarded her quizzically for a moment or two, before replying.

'Shall we just say that I'm her financial adviser and that I'm contemplating going into partnership with her?'

Which probably meant, as she'd already guessed, that he intended to marry Estelle.

His shrewd sapphire eyes did not miss much during their tour of the farmyard and its environs, though the stables seemed to hold Griff's interest longer than anything else; and by the time they returned to the house, Shari was sure he had a very accurate picture of the property and its possibilities. Now she was dreading going back to the drawing-room and finding that her grandmother and Estelle had completed their negotiations, that the irrevocable step had been taken.

Griff Masterson must have sensed something of what she felt; certainly he could have been in no doubt of

Shari's affection for Threlkeld and for her native valley. It had been in the tone of her husky voice, in her lovely eyes, as, unconsciously, she betrayed that she was taking what she believed to be a farewell of everything she loved.

'A property sale isn't the kind of thing to be concluded in five minutes, you know,' he told her, his voice gentle as he paused to take a last, thoughtful look at the stable yard. 'There will have to be a surveyor's report on the house, and my firm will expect me to go into the whole thing pretty thoroughly before we can advise Estelle to buy.'

'You mean there's still a chance she might not buy it?' Shari asked eagerly, hope reborn in her widely spaced, violet eyes turned up to him; but she was immediately downcast once more, as Griff shook his head.

'I wouldn't say that, no. Estelle is a pretty determined woman. She knows what she wants and goes all out for it. There would have to be a very unfavourable report on the property, dry rot, damp, subsidence or something else about the place which she disliked, to make her change her mind. But you could do worse, you know, than have Estell buy it. She's a good business woman and she can well afford to put the place back on its feet.'

'Is she very rich?'

'Very!' he confirmed.

Soberly, Shari led the way back to the drawing-room, her heart as leaden as were her normally winged feet. Despite Griff Masterson's assurances, she didn't want Estelle to be the new owner. An experienced farmer with only restoration and an injection of new finance wouldn't be so bad. But Shari couldn't envisage Estelle as a farmer pure and simple. Only one tiny spark of hope remained to her, the fact that possibly Estelle could be put off by a serious enough disadvantage.

Then a more suitable buyer could be found. For, in her instinctive dislike of the other woman, she had not forgotten her grandmother's urgent need to sell. But she knew that if she could think of something that would prevent this particular woman buying Threlkeld, some opportunity to give her a distaste for the area, she would take it.

From her grandmother's greeting, it seemed that opportunity at least had been granted to her.

'Miss Garner would like to learn more about the area before she comes to a final decision. So I've invited her to stay here with us for a few days. Can I extend the same invitation to you, Mr Masterson?' Abigail Freeman looked less strained than of late; and with a twinge of guilt, Shari sensed in her grandmother a relief that negotiations were at least under way.

Shari looked at Griff for his reaction to her grandmother's offer. He looked pleased, she noted, for, once again that wide, slightly gap-toothed smile lent charm to his rugged features.

'Thank you! I'd be delighted to accept, but on one condition, that you allow us to be paying guests whilst we explore the area!' He raised a silencing hand. 'Please, don't see my offer as an insult. We do appreciate your gesture of hospitality. But let's be practical about this. The extra cash coming in would be useful.'

Though Abigail still made a token protest, Shari knew the offer *was* a relief; and she wondered briefly, if Threlkeld didn't sell, whether they could supplement their income by taking paying guests. She would suggest it to Abigail when they were alone.

'Perhaps,' Griff continued, 'since she seems to know every yard of Beckdale so intimately, your granddaughter would be prepared to act as a guide in our explorations?' Eyes quizzical, he looked at Shari for confirmation. But Estelle immediately demurred.

'Oh, I don't think that will be necessary, darling.'

'I think Mr Masterson is right,' Abigail said quietly. 'The hills around Beckdale can be very stark and wild. A guide who knows the area is an essential. Shari has run wild on them all her life.'

'I can imagine!' Estelle's wry little smile made Shari's hackles rise. For the first time in her life she wanted to be glamorous, assured enough to outface another woman, and her resentment grew proportionately.

There was an appeal in Abigail's voice.

'Shari?'

At first she wanted to protest, but even as she opened her lips to make some excuse, she hesitated. Wasn't this exactly the chance she needed to disenchant the older woman with the countryside? Drive her away from Beckdale?

'All right. I don't mind.' At the casual, unexpectedly meek reply, a sharp sapphire gleam from Griff's eyes gave her the uncomfortable feeling that he at least was suspicious about her apparent readiness to be obliging.

'Good! That's settled,' Abigail Freeman said. 'Shari, would you ask Lily to prepare rooms for our guests?'

Glad to escape, Shari nodded and slipped from the room; then, her errand performed, she went in search of Jimmy, to bring him up to date and to outline her proposed campaign.

'Shari! Don't be daft! It won't change anything. You'll only be postponing the evil moment, and making things harder for your grandmother. You know she's got to sell and it might not be so easy to find another buyer.'

'I know,' she conceded, 'I know we'll have to sell, that I've got to accept it. But I just *know* Estelle Garner is the wrong owner for Threlkeld. She wouldn't fit in. I'd rather almost anyone else bought the place. It's no use arguing. I'm going to try my hardest to put her off.'

'I could warn your grandmother,' Jimmy began, 'not to let you.'

'But you won't,' she said confidently, 'because you wouldn't want to upset her. And besides, if you did, I'd never speak to you again.' It wasn't fair to make use of her friendship with Jimmy, but she had to.

Over dinner that evening her resolution was strengthened, when Estelle, suddenly voluble, began to outline her plans for the Hall, with what Shari considered to be complete disregard for the tender feelings of its present occupants.

'Of course, it will mean a lot of re-structuring.' She was addressing Griff. 'The place is hopelessly old-fashioned. We'll have to extend too, by knocking through into that old barn and putting in extra accommodation, more bathroom facilities.'

Appalled, Shari listened and saw her dismay reflected in her grandmother's face as it became apparent that what Estelle had in mind was nothing less than a large, self-contained holiday complex, with sporting facilities and entertainment, as well as daytime outdoor activities.

'We can convert some of the other outbuildings too, or even throw up a whole new block. It doesn't really matter which. We'll need a ballroom and a games-room naturally, and a restaurant. This dining-room is far too small.' She looked round critically. 'Catering facilities, and I thought a heated swimming-pool, sauna, hair-dressing for the women.'

'Well, that about takes care of the creature comforts,' Griff said, with a glinting smile at Shari which was meant to be conspiratorial, inviting her amusement at such totally feminine luxuries. But she didn't respond. He was part of Estelle's schemes. 'What had you in mind for *outdoors*?'

Estelle shrugged her shoulders, the gesture also making her magnificent breasts rise and fall. She had changed for dinner and her plunging neckline left little to the imagination, all that naked, swelling flesh exposed, no doubt, for Griff's benefit. Shari couldn't help a swift, downward glance at her own more modest proportions. Compared with Estelle, she supposed a man like Griff would find *her* unfeminine. Anyway, she didn't care what he thought. Despite all his attempts to be friendly, he was on the side of the enemy.

'That's your department, darling,' Estelle was saying vaguely. 'I suppose a few frightfully macho things, like rock-climbing? Sailing? I did hear mention of a lake, didn't I?'

'Would you want to keep the farm going?' Griff asked. 'It could be a profitable little sideline, if we could bring methods up to date, inject a little extra finance. Animal husbandry might appeal to some of your guests. I wouldn't mind,' he said slowly, 'dealing with that aspect of it myself.'

'Feel free, darling! Since you'll be living here too, we must keep you happy.'

Shari felt her colour rising hectically. She was convinced there was sexual innuendo in that remark. Griff was far too nice for Estelle, Shari was surprised to find herself thinking, in spite of her determination to dislike them both equally.

'And what about pony-trekking too?' he suggested. Outwardly his manner was quiet, casual even but Shari, looking at him with sudden intentness, detected an underlying eagerness in his voice. Was this where Griff's real interest lay?

Estelle gave him another of the little smiles, which Shari interpreted as implied intimacy.

'Yes, I suppose we must allow you to have your gee-gees too. But practicalities first, darling. We'll simply have to have central heating installed, oil-fired, I thought? Open fires are frightfully picturesque and all that, but not very efficient. I want our guests to feel cosseted.'

Fuel, it seemed, listening to Estelle, would arrive

efficiently, pumped in every six months or so by great tankers. Secretly, Shari smiled, imaging the heavy vehicles negotiating the narrow roads to the valley, a particularly hazardous undertaking in winter, when the fuel would be needed, sometimes an impossible one. She wondered whether she should enlighten Estelle. But no. Estelle was unlikely to listen to her. The other woman must be given a distaste for the area by a practical demonstration of its drawbacks.

A casual remark by Abigail Freeman paved the way.

'Shari, why don't you plan a short fell walk for tomorrow, so that Mr Masterson and Miss Garner can see something of the type of terrain their visitors would be encountering?'

Estelle looked enquiringly at Griff.

'How about it, darling?'

'Not for me. There are one or two matters I'd like to look into, financial aspects concerning the farm and the stableyard. The firm will expect me to do my homework.'

'The firm?' Shari enquired curiously.

'The firm of solicitors that I represent, Estelle's solicitors.' Then, to Estelle, 'But you go by all means. It will give you and Shari a chance to get better acquainted.'

'It does seem unnecessary to drag Miss Freeman away from her own pursuits,' Estelle demurred. She gave Shari a doubtful smile. 'Much as Miss Freeman deplored my mistake, she does *look* scarcely more than a child and so frail! I hardly feel in need of her guidance. I'm an excellent walker, with plenty of stamina.'

'No one doubts that, Miss Garner,' Abigail Freeman said politely, 'but I assure you, it's easier than you might imagine to get lost, whereas Shari knows her way around the fells even in the dark. Slight she may be, but she's very sure-footed and strong.'

'Oh, very well,' and to Shari, 'I presume slacks and

some kind of flat, sensible shoes will be all that's
necessary?'

Next morning, Shari had to turn away to hide a smile at
the sight of what Estelle considered to be 'sensible'
shoes. The flat, open, black-patent slip-ons looked very
elegant with black slacks, their edges knife-creased, and
the white polo-necked sweater, but Shari could
practically guarantee that the other woman would not
return from their expedition looking so immaculate,
and she was forced to squash an inconveniently active
conscience. She *had* to do this for the sake of Threlkeld.
Even the weather was playing into her hands. It had
rained overnight. The fellside would be muddy and
forward progress much impeded.

'Now, just take Miss Garner on a nice easy scramble
to begin with,' Abigail Freeman adjured. 'Remember, *she*
hasn't spent her whole life running about on the
mountainside,' and to Estelle, 'You'll need a weatherproof coat, my dear. March in Lakeland can be very
treacherous.'

'Are you sure you won't come, Griff?' Estelle asked.

'Positive! I thought I'd spend some time getting to
know Jimmy, go through some of the accounts with
him. But if Shari will leave word which route she
intends to take, I daresay Jimmy will be able to guide
me? We may intercept you somewhere along the way?'

Shari was relieved. Griff, she was sure, would have been
less easy to deceive as to what constituted the difference
between a nice easy scramble and the endurance test to
which she intended to submit Estelle; and yet, as she
met the direct straightness of his sapphire-blue eyes,
she felt again that irritating stir of her conscience. After
this morning he was going to have a very poor opinion
of her and though it shouldn't matter to her, oddly that
thought troubled her. After all, what was it to her what
Griff Masterson, an 'off-comer', thought of her?

CHAPTER TWO

WORKMANLIKE in her faded jeans, sweater, light anorak and well-used fell boots, Shari led the way out of the farmyard. Patting the light haversack she carried on her back, she explained,

'I asked Lily to make us up some sandwiches and a flask, just in case we don't get back in time for lunch.' She was quite determined that they wouldn't. She cast an appraising eye at the sky, then transferred her thoughtful gaze to Estelle's notion of a weatherproof coat, a smart woollen blazer, which teamed with the slacks and shoes.

Shari had decided on a route which would lead them immediately into the heart of the fells, by means of a deceptively easy gradient. She didn't want Estelle turning back before she was fully committed. She was careful too, not to set too brisk a pace and she knew that her ploy was working, when Estelle remarked in surprise,

'Why! There's nothing to this fell-walking after all, is there? I can't think what all the fuss is about, people loading themselves up with unnecessary expensive equipment, the tall stories they tell afterwards. All grossly exaggerated, I've always thought, and now I know I was right.'

The lower part of the fell, where it joined the valley floor, was well wooded, the trees extending up to and over the summit, hiding the craggy prospect beyond. Tenuous paths led up to rocky promontories, where, looking back, a bird's-eye view could be obtained of Beckdale and its tiny lake. Higher up still, the valley became remarkably rocky, with low, steep outcrops on every hand. But Shari did not propose to follow that route. Already Estelle seemed a little breathless, and they had not yet reached the terrain that was intended to complete the older woman's disenchantment.

The track which had brought them to the fell-top now turned sharply to traverse the steep fellside, running along the foot of an impressive series of crags.

'Handy, if any of your guests are aspiring mountaineers,' Shari commented.

'You mean people actually climb up those things?' Estelle looked horrified.

'Oh yes!' Shari was airy. 'I've done it myself. When you're more experienced you'll have to try it.'

'Never!' Estelle turned away from the prospect with a shudder and followed Shari down the gentler incline, which descended the far side of the fell, giving them their first view of Brush Gill and the Glencora massif.

Brush Gill, a hanging valley surrounded on all sides by the most incredible crags, was the key to Glencora. Ordinarily, Shari would now have taken the route to the summit. But this was too easy an ascent, pleasant, but not what Shari had in mind for her companion.

'I thought we'd take a look at the Cuckoo's Nest,' she told Estelle, guessing rightly that the innocent-sounding name would appeal.

The Cuckoo's Nest looked like a normal crag, but was far from being so. In times past, a whole rock-face had become dislodged from the fellside, slipped a few feet, then come to rest. The result was a gap between the visible, outer surface of the rocks and the inner core, the final result resembling a series of caves, penetrating into the mountain.

Entry was by way of the Funkhole, known thus because it was not for the faint-hearted. Shari led the way into this very narrow, low gap in the rocks, through which it was just possible to squirm if she removed her rucksack and thrust it before her. She ignored faint sounds of protest from behind, knowing that Estelle would be anxious not to lose her guide. The older woman would be finding the Funkhole something of a claustrophobic experience. It could be an unnerving place if you weren't used to it.

It was necessary now to squirm up a cleft in the bowels of the fell, no more than a few inches wide and about twelve feet high. The agile Shari had made the ascent many times and knew there was no danger of falling; the rock gripped too tightly for that, but anyone of more than modest girth would find the way up to be utterly exhausting, more like pot-holing than climbing. Not without that annoying reminder of guilt, Shari thought of Estelle's generous curves.

'Shari! Shari!' A protesting cry rose from beneath her. 'I can't get up there! Come back!'

'Impossible!' Shari called back. 'It's easier to go on now than to go back.'

She began to wonder if she hadn't gone too far with her prank as she listened to Estelle's panicky attempts, and for the first time she began to feel afraid of the inevitable retribution. Her grandmother would be very angry when she learnt how their guest had been treated, and though Jimmy never lost his temper with her, she didn't relish his disapproval either; and then there was Griff. For some reason, she just dared not think about Griff.

Estelle didn't seem to be making much progress, and fear took on an edge of anger. This stupid, useless woman. Instead of learning her lesson, that Lakeland was not for her and her kind, she was just going to get Shari into probably the worst trouble she'd been in in her whole life.

'Come on!' she shouted impatiently. 'I can't go any further until you get up here, we need my torch to find our way through the caves.'

There was a shrill cry of anguish from below; then

Estelle's voice drifted up to her, afraid, despairing, her cool poise totally cracked.

'I'm stuck! I can't move either way.'

Shari felt herself beginning to tremble. What *had* she done? She honestly hadn't meant *this* to happen. Oh why had she been so foolish as to let her dislike for this woman lead her to such extremes? There were other tough, trying walks that wouldn't have involved actual danger.

'Are you ... are you sure?' she enquired, trying to disguise the tremulousness in her own tone.

'Positive!' A note of angry bewilderment entered the cultivated accents. 'Why, Shari? Why did you do this? You *must* have known what would happen.' Then, on a fading note, 'I *will* get out, won't I? I mean, you can get help? You *must!*' Ending on a high note of hysteria.

Yes, she could get assistance, though it might take some time.

'I'll go for help.' She nearly added 'stay where you are', and struck by the incongruity of the remark, a giggle that was hysterical rather than malicious in origin escaped her; but was heard as mockery by Estelle.

'If I'd known you were such a spiteful little cat ... but when I do get out of here, you'll laugh the other side of your face. Childish! Irresponsible!'

Despite mingled remorse and apprehension, Shari couldn't forbear a retort.

'Careful, or I might leave you there to fend for yourself. It could be months before anyone else comes this way.'

Then she was off, making her way into a gully from which it was possible to enter the rest of the caves. Shari made straight for the exit; but, as she left the final cave, she was confronted by the last person she had expected to see, a grim-faced Griff Masterson, and with him, looking apprehensive, but annoyed too, was Jimmy.

'Shar! You blithering idiot!' Jimmy began with more than usual vehemence, but Griff cut him short, his speech clipped.

'Later! Miss Freeman will get what's coming to her. But first,' sharply, 'where's Estelle?'

Warily edging round him to reach Jimmy's side, Shari's voice was subdued as she said defensively,

'She's stuck! I was just going for help.'

'What on earth possessed you to take her through the Cuckoo's Nest?' Jimmy demanded. 'It's not like you to be so irresponsible. You *know* it's a tricky climb for a beginner.'

'Didn't you bring a rope in your haversack?' Griff snapped.

'Of course,' indignantly, 'I never go climbing without one, but I'm not strong enough to pull Miss Garner up.'

'You should have thought of that,' Griff's displeasure was making her feel more uncomfortable than she had imagined possible, 'before you put her into such a nasty position. Crosthwaite! You know these caves?' And as Jimmy nodded, 'Right, lead the way. I'll probably need your help to draw Estelle up. Shari, your torch please.'

Shari stood feeling useless, watching the men disappear. Griff, she noticed with faint surprise, was very unlike his usually immaculate, tailored self, wearing a pair of ancient corduroys, sweater and anorak and boots which had obviously seen plenty of service. The arrival of the men was very opportune, she had to admit. It would have taken her some time to return to Beckdale for help. But of course, she'd left a note on Jimmy's desk, telling him her eventual destination, and she supposed knowing her as well as he did and knowing something of her plan to discourage Estelle, he had half guessed that she might intend to play some trick on the other woman.

Suddenly she knew she couldn't wait here until the

others emerged. The prospect to which she had looked forward, that of seeing Estelle bedraggled, her cool self-confidence destroyed, no longer seemed attractive. She didn't fear Jimmy's disapproval. He was her friend, would remain so whatever she did. But she dreaded Griff's angry contempt. There had been a controlled wrath in him, subdued at this moment of crisis, but quite likely to break forth again when it was over, and *she* would be the object of that wrath. All at once, her aim was to make herself scarce before Griff reappeared.

Turning on her heel, she scrambled madly for the summit of the crag, traversed a ridge from which she knew she could descend to the head of Littlestrath, following this latter valley back to Pebblethwaite, where it would be possible to get the local taxi service to take her home.

By the time the others had made their way back to Beckdale, tempers might have cooled a little and she would have the advantage of being on home ground.

Perhaps Estelle would have been so unnerved by her experience that she would insist on packing up and leaving straight away, and naturally Griff would have to fall in with Estelle's wishes. It was a pity, she found herself thinking inconsistently as she made her solitary walk, that a nice man like Griff had got himself involved with Estelle Garner. For however much she tried, she couldn't dislike him as she ought. Now, if *he* had been the intending purchaser of Threlkeld, things might not have seemed quite so bad.

'Gran!' Still in her disreputable walking gear, Shari hovered in the doorway of Abigail's elegant parlour.

Mrs Freeman raised horrified eyebrows.

'Darling,' she said despairingly, 'will you *ever* be ladylike, I wonder?'

'If by "ladylike" you mean all paint and perfume and plunging necklines, like Miss Garner, I hope not!'

'Did Miss Garner enjoy her walk?' Abigail enquired, ignoring the outburst. She had long since resigned herself to the fact that Shari was a wild tomboy and would probably remain so until some man came along who was capable of taming her. 'I hope you didn't overtire her?'

Shari shut the door and in a sudden rush collapsed on her knees at Abigail's feet, her violet eyes wide and imploring.

'Oh, Gran! I've done the most *dreadful* thing. I have to tell you first, before *they* do.'

How many times, as a child, had she come here to confess some misdemeanour before retribution in the shape of Lily, or, less often, her father, had caught up with her? Though of late there had been no childish sins to relate, the room still had for her the air of sanctuary, with its panelled walls, the rich polished wood of the dignified Sheraton desk at which her grandmother wrote her letters, the Georgian chairs with their gracefully curved legs and elaborate backs, the Chippendale table, its wood shimmering like glass from Lily's enthusiastic polishing. The impression of a confessional was increased by the small, diamond-paned window, with its pattern of stained glass, which overlooked the small, trim rose garden that was, in summer, Abigail's delight.

Abigail had paled slightly, an anxious hand going to her throat; visions flashed before her eyes of her hasty-tempered, impetuous granddaughter pushing Estelle off a rockface.

'What *have* you done, Shari?'

'Gran, you can't want *her* to buy Threlkeld, she wouldn't fit in, she's not right for the dalesfolk. They'd *hate* what she wants to make of our valley.'

'I know, child,' the old lady said wearily, 'but there's nothing I can do about it. I'm too old and too tired. I have to sell and there aren't many people about with her kind of money who want an isolated farmhouse. But you'd better tell me what you've been up to. I can't stand the suspense.' It was not said jokingly. Abigail was perfectly serious, her expression strained.

'I ... I only wanted to put her off ... honestly. I thought if she took a dislike to the countryside, she ... she'd go away.' Out it came, an incoherent tumble of words, the dance she had led Estelle.

'And you *left* her stuck in that horrible place you've just described?'

Abigail had never been a lover of climbing and walking, preferring the comforts of domesticity, the mountains just a pleasant view through her windows, a source of exhilaratingly clear, fresh air. 'You didn't wait to see if they got her out?' Her tone deplored such cowardice. 'Miss Garner is our *guest*!' The mores of hospitality too had been flouted.

'They'll get her out all right, two strong men pulling her up.' Shari could not keep the scorn out off her voice. 'If she weren't such a rabbit! I've done that climb dozens of times.'

'I *thought* you'd come to me to make a clean breast of things, not to try and justify your behaviour by denigrating Miss Garner.' Any further reproach Abigail might have contemplated was postponed by the sound of footsteps and voices, Estelle's determined, Jimmy's clear voice anxious, placatory, and Griff Masterson's firm, authoritative.

'I suggest, Estelle, that you change and calm down before you speak to Mrs Freeman. As Jimmy says, she's not in the best of health.'

'Shari!' Abigail commanded. 'Open the door and invite Miss Garner and Mr Masterson to come in.'

Slowly, her granddaughter moved to obey, then returned to stand behind her grandmother's chair, holding on to the back of it with fingers that gripped until the knuckles whitened.

'Please sit down, Miss Garner!' Abigail's voice was controlled. 'I understand my granddaughter has behaved very badly.'

'That must be the understatement of the year!' It was said wearily, as Estelle sat on one of Abigail's precious chairs, taking no account of the effect her lacerated and soiled clothing might have upon the pristine upholstery. Shari stared in fascination at the outcome of her mischief, which far exceeded all her expectations.

The expensive black slacks and blazer would not even be fit for a jumble sale now. Stuck fast, yet pulled vigorously from above by two strong young men, something had had to give and the fabric had been no match for rugged rock. The red fingernails were chipped and broken, the red hair in wild disarray.

'Your granddaughter,' Estelle's voice was tremulous, as though delayed shock had now set in, 'damn' near killed me. She's totally irresponsible.'

'Mrs Freeman,' Jimmy intervened desperately, as Abigail's hand fluttered towards her throat. 'There was never any real danger. Shari only meant it as a prank, you know she'd never . . .'

'It's no use trying to cover up for your girlfriend,' Estelle interrupted him. 'You saw the state in which she abandoned me, and thank God, I also have an independent witness. Griff . . . darling?' She held out her hand to the tall blond man, who had remained silent so far, his sapphire gaze clinically intent upon Shari's pale face, noting the anguish in violet eyes, the tremble of the vulnerable mouth.

Jimmy tried again.

'Shari *hadn't* abandoned you, she was on her way to get help.'

Estelle's gaze narrowed on his earnest face.

'Strange that *you* should be so conveniently on the spot. One might almost imagine that you were implicated in her plans.'

Shari hadn't attempted to excuse herself, but now she flew to Jimmy's defence.

'Jimmy knew which way we were going, but that's all. He didn't know I meant to go into the Cuckoo's Nest. If he had he'd have stopped me.'

'Be that as it may,' Estelle retorted, 'you've cooked your goose as far as I'm concerned. Griff had suggested that I keep the pair of you on to work for me. But after this, I just couldn't trust either of you near the class of clientele I expect to get here.'

'Work for *you*?' Shari exclaimed, her face burning, her whole body trembling with a violent, frustrated anger which had no outlet other than Estelle on which to expend itself. 'I suppose you thought you'd be doing me a great favour. Well thanks for nothing. I wouldn't *lower* myself!' It didn't occur to her until afterwards that Jimmy might have been more grateful for the guaranteed continuation of his employment.

'Miss Garner, I . . . I just don't know what to say,' Abigail faltered, 'how to apologise. I . . .'

'I don't *want* anyone to apologise for me!' Shari interrupted. 'Especially not you, Gran!'

'I agree!' For the first time since he had entered the room, Griff spoke. 'I think we've imposed on Mrs Freeman long enough. She's looking tired. Estelle, I suggest you go and change now.' His voice was gentle, coaxing. He paused, then, 'Shari will do her own apologising in due course.' But now the softness of his deep voice did not belie the assurance in it.

'*Shari will not!*' Defiantly, she tried to outface him, despite the unsteadiness in her voice, the compelling glance of his eyes.

'Oh, yes, Shari will!' he contradicted, emphasising each word, not with anger, but with a determination which had Shari looking for some avenue of escape, afraid that somehow he *was* capable of coercing her, not by superior strength but by the force of his will.

'And I'll tell you *why* you're going to apologise,' he continued, 'but not here. It's time we left your grandmother to rest.'

Estelle had gone, her annoyance only slightly abated, but her need to reassume her normal sophisticated elegance taking priority over everything else; an embarrassed Jimmy had left unobserved, and yet the room still seemed suffocatingly overcrowded. Shari began to edge towards the door.

'I'd better go and get changed too.' As she slipped into the hallway, she thought she had effected her escape. But Griff was close behind her and somehow he had managed to block her way to the staircase.

'That can wait!' he told her. Then, wryly, 'I don't think your need is as urgent as Estelle's.'

'No!' she retorted. 'But then I don't find it necessary to go round looking like a fashion plate. I *know* what's suitable wear.'

'Then wouldn't it have been kinder of you to advise Estelle?' he interrupted, a touch of sternness in the rebuke. 'You're not a child, so you inform me, yet you seem to behave like one.'

To her mortification, Shari felt her lips tremble, knowing that his remark was justified.

'Come on!' he commanded, but in a kinder tone. 'We can't talk here. Let's go outside.'

Without waiting for a reply, negative or otherwise, he took hold of her arm, just above the elbow, his grip hard even through the thick wool of her sweater, and urged her towards the side door, out into the stable yard. He did not relax his grip, as he steered her along the line of empty loose-boxes, and at first his interest seemed to lie in these, giving Shari a badly needed chance to steady herself.

'How long is it since you had horses at Threlkeld? Apart from your own mare, and the Shire?'

'I don't remember, before I was born I think.'

'Hmm!' He threw open one of the doors and looked inside, drawing her after him. 'These aren't in such bad shape, considering. How would you like to see these loose-boxes full of horses again?'

'Horses belonging to Estelle?' Shari said bitterly, trying to turn away. 'What do *you* think?' But she was not to escape him so easily.

'Yes, Estelle, we'll come to your treatment of her in a moment. But first, for your information, the horses wouldn't belong to her, they'd be mine.'

'Oh?' Shari was still uninterested, despite her love of horses. She wouldn't be here to see the animals, no matter what their ownership.

'But you like horses?' he pressed.

Of course she did. She'd been able to ride almost before she could walk; but now, if she had to leave Threlkeld, she might not even be able to keep Rainbow. Sharply, she told Griff so.

'Under certain circumstances,' he said slowly and carefully, his eyes watchful on her unhappy face, 'you might be able to stay, to keep your little mare.'

'Under certain circumstances?' Her head jerked up, elevating the chin that annoyingly still had a tendency to wobble. 'You mean if I crawl to your girlfriend? No, thank you, very much!' She turned, intending to leave the stable, to leave him, needing to find a place where she could indulge her misery unobserved.

The preventive hand he flung out missed her arm, grasping her fingers instead, and he held on steadily despite her struggles, pulling her further into the loose-box, one foot kicking the lower half of the door shut. Against this he leant, effectively barring her only means of escape.

He had released her hand, but she stood stock still, shocked into silence, waiting for an end to the very odd sensations that were running from her fingers to the rest of her body. She seemed to feel an actual tingling where his hand had made contact. Why should Griff's touch make her feel so odd? She made a little choking sound, pressing her fingers into her other hand, as if by this she could stifle the effect of his grasp.

'What is it? I'm sorry! Did I hurt you?' He was so close that she could see herself reflected in those sapphire-blue eyes.

'No ... no, really,' she said, trying to manoeuvre her hand behind her back, so that he couldn't take it to inspect it for damage. But her reactions seemed to be slow, as if she were mesmerised, and he was too swift for her, capturing the hand, stroking it between his warm, calloused ones, and that odd sensation returned.

She was shaking so violently that she felt it must be apparent to him. What on earth was the matter with her? She had never felt like this before in her life, this feeling of malaise, as though she were sickening for something, pulses racing, heart beating erratically, a kind of nausea that was half fear, half excitement.

He *had* noticed her strange reaction, because he was watching her now, intently, his own expression oddly arrested, and his appraisal was unnerving her. She *must* pull herself together. He would be wondering why her flow of angry words had dried up so suddenly. She hadn't even answered his question.

'Shari!' His grasp on her hand tightened. 'You didn't let me finish. The horses would belong to me.' The ball of his thumb moved as though absently against her palm. 'And I'd like you to work for *me*, help with the pony-trekking.'

'What is this, Mr Masterson?' Again she tried to free herself, her nerves still rawly on edge from the strange sensations she experienced. 'Charity?'

'No!' he said violently. 'And I wish you'd call me Griff. I wouldn't think of offering you such an insult, you'd *earn* your wages. It just seemed a practical idea, to our mutual benefit. I wanted to keep young Jimmy on too. I'm very impressed by his grasp of the finances of this place.'

For the first time the full extent of her irresponsibility was brought home to her. Her actions had lost Jimmy *his* job, which, according to Griff, he might otherwise have kept. She had to put in a word for Jimmy. Experimentally she tugged at her hand again, but he seemed determined not to free her and she was forced to face him as she made her plea.

'Please, don't let her sack Jimmy. She'll listen to you. Tell her she's got it wrong. He didn't know anything about the trick I played on her; and he *needs* this job, not just for his sake, but for his grandmother's. Lily's getting near retirement age.'

'It's not a forlorn hope for either of you if,' he paused significantly, 'if you're prepared to do the right thing, to apologise to Estelle, and you *do* owe her an apology. If so, I think I may be able to persuade her.'

'Well, I'm not prepared,' she snapped tearfully, 'not to her. She's not wanted here at Threlkeld.'

'By you? Perhaps not. But if you want me to back you up as far as Jimmy's concerned, that's what you've got to do. And have you thought of your grandmother in all this? The worry and responsibility of keeping up a large property? Without the means to do so? And what about the new money our guests would inject into Beckdale?'

'Of course I've thought of my grandmother, that's the whole point. How do you think she'd feel, seeing her old home changed out of all recognition, and besides, a fat lot the dalesfolk would see of the money with your girlfriend's self-contained holiday complex soaking it all up.'

'What about the employment we could offer the younger members of the community, like Jimmy? So that they needn't drift away from the valley to earn a living?'

'All right! All right!' Shari cried in exasperation. 'So you've got an answer for everything, except Miss Garner. It wouldn't be so bad if somebody less objectionable wanted to buy the place, somebody who would leave it as it is, instead of opening it up to tourists, ruining the peace, the beauty.'

'I wonder,' he said consideringly, 'why you've taken quite such a violent dislike to Estelle. She's not a bad sort, but you got off on the wrong foot with her, didn't give her a chance. Could it be that you're jealous of her for some reason?'

'Jealous?' Shari's voice actually squeaked, such was her outrage. 'What's *she* got that I should be jealous of?' She found she didn't care at all for his championship of the other woman.

'The money to restore Threlkeld? Looks? Nice clothes? Her sheer femininity perhaps?' His eyes submitted Shari to a comprehensive inspection. 'If it weren't for that glorious long black hair of yours, you could be mistaken for a boy.'

'Then I'm glad,' Shari cried fiercely. 'I'd rather look as *I* do than like *her*. I despise women who dress as she does, in tight clothes, flaunting their ... their ...'

'Breasts and hips?' he finished for her softly, his eyes moving thoughtfully over those parts of *her* body, successfully disguised by the long bagginess of a Herdwick wool sweater. 'You're afraid even to say the words, aren't you? Why are you so ashamed of being female, Shari? Don't you know that, with a little care and attention *you* could be very attractive, very feminine. Your hair ...' He reached out as if to touch it and she shied away like a startled pony.

'Damn my hair! I'll go into Keswick tomorrow and get it cut, shorter than *yours*,' she said, disdainfully, eyeing the corn-gold hair that grew from a central peak and down, too close in her opinion, to his collar.

'*Don't you dare!*'

She did not manage to evade him this time and his fingers plunged into the lustrous black waves, grasping a handful of them. For a moment he stared at her almost wonderingly, then pulled her towards him, hard up against his strong, sinewy body. She felt a quiver run over her ... revulsion, of course. How *dare* he manhandle her like this? She was aware now of his hand stroking the despised hair, his cheek resting against its soft silkiness. 'Don't you dare commit such a desecration!'

He shouldn't be doing this. What *was* he doing exactly? And she shouldn't be permitting it; but she seemed unable to move of her own accord. What would Estelle ...?

'Let me go,' she whispered.

'I don't believe you've ever been held in a man's arms before,' he said wonderingly.

He must be able to tell by the uncontrollable shuddering that racked her. How juvenile she must seem to him in comparison to the ultra-sophisticated Estelle, who would know what to do now, how to respond, or how to escape. All at once her familiar world had become chaotic. If this had been Jimmy or one of the farm lads, she would have pushed them away with a jesting word or two. This ... this ... inertia she felt was ... was almost ... *pleasant*! Something was happening to her, but what?

'Please, please, Griff, let me go ...' It was a feeble protest at best and it wasn't really surprising that he ignored it. His hand left her hair and slid down the length of her back, leaving delicious tremors in its wake. His blond head bent lower, his lips pushing aside the heavy fall of her hair, seeking, finding and nibbling gently on her earlobe. Passively, she permitted the delicate grazing of his teeth, experiencing for the first time in her life the weakening waves of warm sensuousness. She gave a little moan. She didn't understand herself. This was the kind of thing she had always despised as 'soppiness'. And yet, without her being aware of it, her body had become pliant, allowing Griff to mould it against his own. Tentatively, wondering at her own daring, at this new experience, she felt her hands, apparently with a will of their own, actually slide up over his broad shoulders, to the nape of his neck; the hair she had disparaged was virile to her touch, a tactile pleasure that stirred still more unfamiliar feelings deep within her. What was she doing? *Why* was she doing it? She ... must ... stop ...

'Have you ever been kissed, Shari?' His voice, she thought, sounded uncertain for him, even a little unsteady. Sleepily, curiously, she lifted her face to look at him, her worried violet eyes meeting sapphire ones, hazy with some emotion she did not recognise, but which seemed to increase her own confusion.

He took the little movement of her head as one of submission and before she could avoid them, his lips came down on to hers, moved over her mouth in a gentle yet demandingly persistent way that made her feel strangely helpless. At first her lips were stiff, unaccustomed, but he went on kissing her, softly, teasingly, coaxing her to part them, until some untutored instinct prompted a response in her. She could scarcely believe what was happening to her. At last, just as she was lost to all other considerations, he drew his mouth away, slowly, as if he had to force himself to do it.

'No,' he murmured. 'No one *has* ever kissed you.' His voice was husky, awed. 'I feel very privileged to be the first.'

An unpleasant kind of irritation was running through her, which, if she had been more experienced, she would have recognised as withdrawal symptoms, the crying out of newly awakened senses; but it made her retort sharply, as he released her, putting her firmly away from him, as someone resisting a temptation.

'But I bet *I'm* not the first woman *you've* kissed.'

'Naturally not,' he confirmed, a mocking note in his voice, and she found herself almost wishing he *had* denied it. She did not rationalise the wish, nor did she comprehend its meaning. She just knew that she felt her anger rising.

'No, of course not!' Her voice cracked huskily on the words. 'I wonder what Estelle would say, if she could have seen you just now? Oh,' desperately, 'why don't you go away, both of you, and leave us alone! *You* don't belong here any more than she does.'

'For all that,' he told her, his manner serious, 'I intend to stay, so you may as well get used to the idea. And I still want you to work for me.'

'I go where my grandmother goes and *she* won't want to stay here and see what you make of her house.'

'On the contrary.' He sounded very assured. 'She's decided, if the sale goes through, to buy that empty cottage in the village. As you reminded me, your Mrs Crosthwaite is anxious to retire and she'll be going with your grandmother. It seems an ideal solution.'

'Gran is going to *stay* in Beckdale?' Shari was incredulous.

'Is that so strange? After living here for upwards of fifty years? It's a mistake to uproot oneself entirely at her age.' His words repeated exactly what she had said to Jimmy, but she hadn't expected Griff Masterson to concern himself with that. 'It would be a great relief to your grandmother, yours and Jimmy's, to think that you were still close by, and I think you'd enjoy working with the ponies.' His sapphire eyes took on a distant look. 'I have all kinds of plans, Shari.' His tone changed, became almost urgent, as if it really *mattered* to him, she thought wonderingly. 'It wouldn't be *so* bad, would it? Working for *me*?'

'I ... I suppose not,' she said slowly, grudgingly, almost relenting, though she didn't know why she

should. 'But,' her lips set obstinately, 'I still wouldn't
take orders from *her*!'

'Oh, Shari, Shari!' There was half amusement, half
exasperation in his laugh. '*How* old are you? What a
child you still are! Look, the outdoor activities will be
my sole responsibility and you'd be working for me and
no one else. Does that suit you?'

Still half reluctantly, she nodded.

'I suppose so.'

'But my condition stands,' he went on and now he
was utterly serious and she knew what was coming.
'You must apologise to Estelle. No, don't jump down
my throat,' as she showed every sign of breaking into
angry speech. 'If you're honest with yourself, you'll
admit she's *entitled* to an apology and if things are
going to run harmoniously there mustn't be any
friction, between *anyone*.'

He was right, but for a moment or two she continued
to stare at him mutinously, lips clamped together, and
he reached out a finger, its skin slightly rough, to trace
the outline of that stubborn mouth, leaving a tingling
trail in the finger's wake, causing an aching sigh to
escape her lips.

'Come on, Shari,' his voice was insidiously coaxing
and she felt bewildered by her desire to please him, 'just
for me, hmm?'

Why was she obeying the dictates of a man she had
known only a few hours? Shari wondered, as she made
her way back towards the house, a man who had
seemed in no doubt that she *would* obey. She found she
was rather frightened of this influence he seemed to
have assumed over her and yet she knew she would do
as he had asked, she would apologise. Not just because
of him, but because she knew she *had* overstepped the
mark with her unkind prank. But, clear-headed, now
that she was out of his disturbing aura, she knew he
must not be permitted to kiss her again. It had been

wrong of *him*, weak of *her* to allow it. It had been sheer insanity. Suppose Estelle ever found out? What would happen to harmony then? There would be hell to pay from the other woman. Griff belonged to her.

She had hated every moment of the humiliating necessity, she thought a few days later. How Estelle must have enjoyed seeing her eat humble pie. Shari had gritted her teeth and gone through with it. Her reward came from seeing the relaxation of tension in Abigail Freeman's face and, less understandably, Griff's warm smile of approval.

'I accept your apology, Shari,' Estelle said in those hatefully cultured accents which irritated Shari's ear. 'But you're getting away very lightly don't you think?'

'I'm inclined to agree with you, Estelle.'

Shari's dark head swung round in astonishment and she stared disbelievingly at Griff. She'd thought that so far as he was concerned, the matter would be closed, once she'd apologised.

'I think,' Griff continued thoughtfully, his eyes meeting Shari's reproachful violet glare, 'that *I* may have a suitable penance for Shari to perform.'

'Oh?' This time Estelle looked sharply at him. 'And what might that be?'

Griff leant towards her, his mouth seeking amidst the auburn hair for Estelle's ear as he had sought *hers*, Shari thought with a reminiscent quiver that brought unexpected pain in its wake and a swift, unreasonable feeling of resentment. Why should *she* care how he drooled over his girlfriend? He murmured a few words and Shari watched Estelle's face change, a smile cross the vividly painted features, her hazel eyes veering briefly in Shari's direction as she gave a little laugh of pure amusement.

'Very appropriate.'

Shari had waited tremulously for the pronouncement

of her sentence, but to her surprise no more had been said on the subject. A day or two passed in trepidation and then, insensibly, she had relaxed. Griff must have forgotten his threat.

'Since Estelle has decided that fell-walking is definitely not her forte, it seems it's up to me to plan some routes for our future guests.' Griff said this one morning over breakfast. 'Would you be willing to act as *my* guide, Shari?'

'Are you sure you can trust me?' she said with a trace of bitterness, though the thought of a day on her beloved fells filled her with exhilaration, that strangely was not lessened by the thought of having to take Griff, one of the unwanted 'off-comers', with her.

'Quite sure!' He sounded amused. 'Can you be ready in half an hour?'

'I can be ready in ten minutes, *I* don't have to paint my face six inches deep before I appear in public.' She didn't look at Estelle as she spoke, keeping her expression blandly innocent, but she heard the sharply indrawn breath and knew that the taunt had gone home, even though Estelle had no proof that it had been meant as such. But Griff too was aware of her meaning and after one defiant try, Shari's eyes fell before the steady glance of his and she felt ashamed of her cheap repartee.

There was no verbal reaction from Estelle and stealing a glance through veiling lashes, she saw an odd little smile on the older woman's face. Retaliation had been planned, she felt sure, but in what form? Obviously Estelle was not to be its administrator. Shari and Jimmy were now officially Griff's responsibility, Estelle having, to Shari's amazement, agreed to them staying on under his supervision.

CHAPTER THREE

'You won't mind if *I* lead?' Griff enquired.

He was wearing the shabby corduroys again, a thick sweater under an anorak and the well-worn boots. She wondered where he had borrowed those.

It was one of those typically gorgeous, sun-blessed spring mornings, the pure, unpolluted air displaying to perfection Beckdale's gleaming lake, which reflected the heights encircling it and giving a crisp edge to the distant views, the craggy skyline. The fells were alive with sparkling becks, still full with the recently melted snows of winter and the lower slopes of the mountainside were splashed with yellow gorse.

Their path commenced just beyond the entrance to the farmyard and Griff set a steady but brisk pace, speaking little, concentrating his efforts. Shari had no fears of not being able to keep up with him. She was willing to bet, since he was no dalesman, that *she'd* be leading by the end of the day.

He was heading for Blawdale Ridge an easy scramble. Pausing for a moment, as she always did, to look back with affection on the lush green of the sloping fields around Threlkeld Hall, Shari was incensed, when Griff enquired,

'Going too fast for you?'

'Of course not!' She caught up with him, matching him stride for stride, and before long they had gained five hundred feet of elevation to the first of the summits. He changed direction slightly now, not following the route Shari would have predicted, but making a scramble across steep scree and into a deep cleft, where an almost vertical cliff barred their way, eleven or twelve feet high.

'We'd better turn back,' Shari suggested. She'd been eager to make Estelle lose face, but somehow she didn't want to see Griff making a fool of himself.

'Whatever for?' He launched himself at the obstacle; and while Shari held her breath, surmounted it with a surprising lack of difficulty.

Shrugging, she followed him. If he *wanted* to end up in the same condition as Estelle that was his look-out. But in any case he wouldn't be able to proceed much further in this direction, which led only to Bendrigg, one of the most taxing ascents even for the experienced; and Shari decided, since Griff was heading straight for it, that she must warn him.

'It's a lot harder than it looks,' she ventured.

'Good! I like a challenge, don't you?' He didn't wait for her answer, but pressed on, his pace in no way diminished, over a stretch of scree. Attempting to keep up with him, Shari slipped and for a moment lay prostrate on the stones, the breath knocked from her body. Annoyingly, she heard Griff calling back to her. 'Need any help?'

'No!' she called back. She was grimly determined not to be outwalked by an off-comer, a novice to her mountains.

Bendrigg was a grim place, even in spring and summer, barren of everything that grew, a rocky wilderness, its final endurance test a tall slit of a chimney, blocked by chockstones, the effect being that of trying to climb a stairway from which the treads had been removed. It was a very tiring climb even for the young and fit. Doggedly, Shari gritted her teeth and followed the seemingly inexhaustible man ahead of her, climbing, gripping, searching for crevices, working slowly into position, then jerking forward. The ascent seemed never-ending, but at last she hauled herself over the final edge and lay exhausted on the top of the peak.

'Need a rest, do you?' Griff sounded incredulous. 'It's

a bit early for lunch too, a bit exposed up here. I thought we'd eat lower down.'

'No,' she said, with forced cheerfulness. 'I don't need a rest, just catching my breath, lead on.'

Griff *must* have done some climbing before. Why hadn't he mentioned it, instead of giving her the impression that he was a raw beginner?

They came down off Bendrigg to encounter a wide barrier of thick, yellow gorse separating them from Ramsdale, the neighbouring valley to Beckdale. Shari looked about her for an alternative route, but Griff, undeterred, plunged into the golden barbs. Grimly now, Shari followed. The gorse scratched and clawed at her clothing and tender skin; but a rising suspicion put iron into her soul. Occasionally she stumbled over concealed roots and hidden rocks. Totally exhausted and unable even for the sake of her pride to hide it, she scrambled out of the gorse and flung herself down on the greensward overlooking Ramsdale tarn.

Griff came to sit beside her. He looked as fresh as when they had started out, his breathing even and untroubled. Shari felt and knew that she looked a mess, hair and clothing dishevelled, her face bright red and moist from her exertions.

'You did that on purpose!'

A lazy, teasing smile transformed his craggy features, increasing their attractiveness.

'You guessed!'

She lunged at him, as she would have done at Jimmy in similar circumstances, fists and feet flailing, overcome by a rage that could only find relief in physical violence, determined on ruffling his insufferable composure. But, laughing aloud, he fended her off easily, holding her slender wrists in an iron grasp, one heavy, booted leg weighing down both of hers.

'Well then, do you consider you've been suitably punished?'

'Oh!' Mortified, she hurled the accusation at him. 'This is what you and Estelle were whispering about! You thought you could avenge your girlfriend by trying to walk me into the ground. Well, you didn't succeed!' She tore free of him and jumped to her feet. 'We've a good few miles to go yet, but you won't hear *me* complaining. I hope those boots you've borrowed give you blisters. You shouldn't wear other people's fell-boots.' Brave words, but the flesh was not as willing as the spirit. The sudden jumping up, following upon the exertion of the past few hours, was the last straw and she felt giddiness swamp her. She swayed and would have fallen but for Griff's prompt action, catching her and lowering her gently to the ground once more.

'Shari?' His voice was anxious. 'Are you all right? I'm sorry, perhaps I did carry things a bit too far. Here, lie down.' He had pulled off his quilted jacket and now he rolled it up, placing it beneath her neck as a pillow.

She could feel him leaning over her, concerned; could imagine the expression on his face as clearly as if she saw it. Already she felt much better, but determinedly she kept her eyes closed. Let him feel the guilt she'd been made to feel over Estelle. But a black feeling of depression settled over her. Recently she had begun to think that things might not be so bad at all, with Griff in part control of Threlkeld. She'd even begun to believe that Griff *liked* her a little; and albeit reluctantly, *she* had begun to like *him*, not in any silly way, of course, she assured herself. After all, he would be marrying Estelle some day.

But it had all been a pose, his friendship, while he'd bided his time to take Estelle's revenge for her. She tried to kindle anger that would burn away the heavy mists of depression, but it was no good, and in spite of all her efforts two painful tears squeezed themselves out from under her eyelids. And Griff saw them.

'Shari? Oh, love, look, I'm sorry I was such a brute.

I've worn you out, haven't I?' There was real contrition in his voice and she felt a calloused finger brush away the tears. That only made things worse, made way for more to follow and in a sudden access of mortification, that he should witness her uncharacteristic weakness, she tried to roll away, to hide her face in the short, sheep-cropped turf. But he prevented the movement.

'Shari!' There was a low, endearing note in his deep voice, its inflection playing oddly on her tattered nerves. One confining arm came around her, curving the bones of her shoulder, pulling her towards him, the powerful body comforting yet also unnerving in its proximity. 'I didn't mean to really hurt you.'

He hadn't hurt her physically, which was what *he* meant, or course, but he had hurt that vulnerable, inner part of her, the part that lay beneath the outward, don't-carish, tomboy exterior. It hurt that *he* should want to make her look foolish.

Then all was forgotten as his mouth brushed her damp eyelids, her cheeks, and she experienced a sensation that savoured of a warning, vague, indescribable, but nonetheless troublesome. His lips moved down to part hers, warm, gently probing, and a strange, restless feeling took hold of her body, so that, without intending to, she found herself responding ardently, suddenly clinging to him. His hand curved around the sensitive nape of her neck, sweetly caressive, each soft touch sending a quiver along her spine. She murmured something protestingly incoherent against his mouth, as she felt sudden tremors disturb the limbs pressed against hers. Immediately he pushed her a little away from him, his breathing unsteady, his hand moving to tilt up her chin, so that she had to meet his gaze. Violet eyes wide and doubtful, she scanned his features and saw him smile, a smile that served to set her pulses overreacting again.

'You're very sweet, Shari!' he sighed. 'And, in some

ways, so very young.' He rolled away and stood up, his
back half turned on her, gazing into the far distance, at
the rearing, majestic heads of the mountains. 'I learnt to
climb in Austria,' he said, almost as if to himself. 'It's a
beautiful country, but this is just as noble, just as
challenging, just as spell-binding.'

Shari sat up, the sweet chains of lethargy cast off, as
she bristled with renewed indignation.

'You're a mountaineer . . . a *real* mountaineer? You
never told me! And you let me . . . oh!' Words failed
her.

He turned towards her, his attractive smile wry.

'These boots,' he held up one foot, 'have climbed,
among other places, in Austria *and* in Switzerland. I'm
sorry, Shari. Can you forgive me for deceiving you?'

'What's to forgive?' she said sharply, all her hurt
remembered. She scrambled to her feet. 'You and
Estelle planned to take me down a peg, and you've
succeeded. You'll be able to have a good laugh together
at my expense. I just hope you're satisfied!'

'In no way,' he said quietly, obscurely, and she stared
at him incredulously. Surely he didn't contemplate
further reprisals? But then he continued briskly, 'Let's
call a truce, put all that behind us now, shall we?' He
held out his hand and after a moment's hesitation, she
took it. After all, her quarrel was not really with him.
But she was wary now, on her guard. He'd been clever,
but he wouldn't find it so easy to make a fool of her
another time. 'And now, shall we eat?'

There was something rather intimate, Shari
discovered, about two people drinking from the same
cup. Beneath her lashes, she watched to make sure that
he did not see her deliberately use the same rim that his
mouth had touched, a foolish little whim, but somehow
pleasurable.

It was an ideal picnic spot. At their backs was the
mountain, from which came the elusive call of the

cuckoo; the first this year, surely? The scent of the gorse was in their nostrils. In the gardens of cottages some way below them, the dancing gold was that of early daffodils. Most of the trees were still without their leaves, but the birch had its first delicate shimmer of green and soon ash, oak and beech would follow its lead.

Although snow still showed on the tops, in the last few days Lakeland seemed to have undergone a sudden change, the arrival of spring. Was it this that seemed to Shari to have brought a lifting of her spirits?

But the euphoria didn't last. Would this sylvan beauty remain unblemished if Estelle had her way? Would Ramsdale and Beckdale take on the appearance of other beauty spots that had been 'discovered' by tourists? She sighed.

'A penny for them?' Griff offered, as he packed discarded wrappers into his haversack. He listened thoughtfully to her reply. 'Yes. I take your point. We'll certainly have to see that our visitors are "educated" into good habits. Litter is a hazard to livestock and I've been thinking,' his voice was suddenly boyishly eager, 'that we ought to have a dairy herd. There are sheep enough, but the lower-lying land is suitable for cattle.'

'Do you know anything about farming?' After what she had learnt of this man today, it would not surprise her if he revealed other hidden talents.

'Enough.' He grinned, that piercingly sweet flash of white teeth in his tanned face. 'My family have always been farmers. I grew up on a farm, in Herefordshire.'

It was the first time he had mentioned his origins, or anything at all personal about himself and Shari's interest quickened.

'But *you're* not a farmer?'

'No.'

'It sounds as if you're contemplating becoming one?' she probed.

'Maybe, it depends . . . on certain things.' He smiled at her quizzically.

Presumably on whether Estelle went through with the purchase of Threlkeld. She wondered when exactly they planned to get married. It must be this unpleasant reminder that soon Threlkeld would no longer be home to her and her grandmother that made her snap sarcastically.

'And I suppose you know all about horses too?'

'About one particular breed of horses, yes. But I know very little about your fell-ponies, and that's one of the things I need to find out, before I know if my scheme is viable.'

'Are you thinking of fell-ponies for the trekking?' Again that unwilling stir of interest, enthusiasm.

'Yes, though that's only part of it. I thought they'd be suitable for the terrain, sure-footed. Would you agree?'

Shari nodded, thinking of the sturdy, dark, long-maned ponies of Lakeland. Once they had been 'wild' and there had been fears that they might die out; but this disaster had been averted by a few horse-lovers, keen on conserving the breed.

'How does one go about getting hold of, say a dozen or so of these ponies?'

'Simple. You contact a local breeder; your girlfriend's uncle for one.' Sarcastically, 'I'm surprised you didn't know that.'

'As yet, I haven't had the pleasure of meeting Mr Garner.'

'Then perhaps it's time you *did* get to know your prospective in-laws.'

'*You'll* introduce me, will you?'

'Surely that's up to Estelle?'

'Not really, since my immediate concern with Mr Garner will be to look over his horses, not to have *him* look *me* over. How well do you know him?'

'Very well, actually. He's always been a sort of honorary uncle to *me*. He taught me to ride, and everything I know about the mountains.'

'Then he did a grand job,' Griff said warmly, 'at least so far as your mountaincraft is concerned. I haven't seen you ride yet.' He rose and pulled her to her feet. 'You came out of today's exercise very well. You're a real sport! And you're such a little slip of a thing!' It was said wonderingly, admiringly. If she hadn't known differently, she might have thought . . . affectionately.

She flushed at this unexpected praise, at the look in his eyes, increasing her lovely, high, natural colour. Did he ever pay such compliments to Estelle, she wondered wistfully. Unlikely. His praise of *her* would take a totally different form, that of her shapely figure and sophisticated beauty.

For the first time in her life, Shari found herself regretting her boyish figure, her very ordinary features. She was totally unaware of the beauty of spirit that shone through the lovely luminescence of her skin, from the depths of her violet eyes, transforming her grave little face into something far more unforgettable than classic features and the gilding of cosmetics.

'We're not far from Charlie's farm now,' she told Griff, in an attempt to cover her confusion, for he was still looking at her with that certain indefinable expression in his eyes. 'We could call in if you like.'

'No, we've still a fair distance to go and *you've* had enough for one day.' He tucked his arm through hers. 'Lean on me if you want to.' As she obeyed, Shari swallowed and hoped the fact that he had disturbed her again was not apparent. 'Tell you what!' The smile that seemed more and more often recently to light his face, broke out again. 'We'll go tomorrow. It'll make an excuse for another day out.'

Shari found herself pondering on this remark as they trudged homeward, more slowly now, out of consideration for her fatigue. Did Griff mean that he *wanted* an excuse to go out with her again?

'Wouldn't you rather take Estelle?' she said abruptly. Such a long time had elapsed since the suggestion that had sparked off her question, that Griff looked puzzled for a second, then:

'Is *that* what you've been brooding about all this time?' he said laughingly. 'And here was I thinking you were asleep on your feet.' His teasing smile vanished as she turned anxious, violet eyes up to him, her expression earnest.

'Surely, you *ought* to be taking *her*?'

He stopped in his tracks, looking down, placing a silencing finger on her soft lips.

'Listen, pint-size!' He made it sound like an endearment. 'It's *you* I want with me. Estelle knows nothing about horses and likes them even less.'

'And yet she doesn't mind you having them about the place?'

'So long as she doesn't need to go near them.' He moved on, linked with her again. 'So, are you coming with me?' And before she could answer, 'Come to think of it, as my future stable girl, it's your duty. I think I'm entitled to insist.'

Since he put it that way, why *should* she refuse? Her debt was paid, in full. Tomorrow, they would be going out as colleagues, friends even. It was not often that Shari's face melted into a whole-hearted smile, but when it did something quite spectacular happened. Now she gave Griff the benefit of that smile, mischievous, puckish, provocative, a lovely, wicked twinkle in the violet eyes.

'And *I* don't think I can possibly refuse such a pressing invitation.'

As he met her gaze, there was a slight stutter in his stride and she heard his sharp intake of breath; but all he said was 'good', an unusually monosyllabic utterance for him. And now, as they completed their homeward walk, it was Griff who seemed sunk in silence.

For once, instead of bouncing out of the house in the first clothes that came to hand, Shari took pains with her appearance. She didn't possess any skirts, but instead of the shabby jeans she donned a trim pair of slacks and a matching jacket over a silky, polo-necked sweater, instead of the usual rough-textured wool. She tried not to see the look of incredulous pleasure on her grandmother's face and failed entirely to see the amused, slightly speculative glance from Estelle. But if she expected Griff to go overboard with compliments, she was disappointed.

'Hmm. Well, yes, it's an improvement,' was his only comment, but something in the sapphire-blue eyes told her that her efforts hadn't been wasted, that he wasn't as unappreciative as he sounded, and she felt a little glow of well-being.

Charlie was delighted, as always, to see Shari and she felt very guilty about her churlish treatment of him at their last meeting. He was pleased also to hear the nature of their errand; and only too happy to have an opportunity of showing off his horseflesh.

'They're larger than I expected,' Griff said with satisfaction. 'Thirteen or fourteen hands?'

Most of the ponies were black or brown, with manes and tails grown long and shaggy. They looked strong and were certainly active, with well-feathered legs. They were dark, wild, almost fierce looking, but, as Shari well knew, were the most docile of creatures.

Griff explained what he had in mind for any ponies he bought and Charlie nodded approvingly.

'He couldn't do better, could he, Shari love? These beasts are the surest footed in the country, and, for their size, probably the strongest. They'll get you over almost any terrain you care to mention bar a vertical rockface.' He laughed. 'Sliding scree, steep slopes, tussocky going, bogland, you'll never see one of these beauties take a fall.'

'And they'd be up to carrying even adults, over fairly long distances?' Griff queried.

'Put sixteen stone up on one of these fellows and he'll hardly feel it,' Charlie asserted proudly. 'They can do a day's hard graft on a farm too, even ploughing.'

'How many mares have you got available for sale? Within say the next two or three months?'

'Half a dozen at the most. As you can see, mine's only a small herd and I don't want to sell off all my breeding potential. How many were you wanting?' On hearing that Griff had twelve ponies in mind as a start, he continued: 'A dozen, eh? Well, that shouldn't be any problem. Fellow I know, over Keswick way, should be able to let you have the other six. Want me to give you his name and telephone number?'

Their business temporarily concluded, Charlie insisted that Shari and Griff come back to the house for a coffee and a bite to eat.

'Can't let your boyfriend get away without trying the missus's shortbread,' he told Shari.

She flushed scarlet and opened her mouth to explain, to introduce Griff properly, but a heavy hand descended on her shoulder, exerting a firm, silencing pressure, as Griff blandly accepted the invitation for both of them.

'Why didn't you *tell* him?' she demanded afterwards, as they left the Garner household. 'He's going to find out sooner or later about you and Estelle, and then it'll be very embarrassing, for *all* of us.'

'Will it?' he asked enigmatically. 'Did *you* find it embarrassing? Being taken for my girlfriend? *Would* that be embarrassing?'

Her colour flaring again, she stammered,

'N . . . no . . . n . . . not if it were . . . true. But it isn't, and you *should* have told him so. Why didn't you?'

'Didn't it occur to you,' Griff answered smoothly, 'that I wouldn't want him to think I was after any favours as a future relative? I intend to pay him a fair price for his animals.'

'Oh! I see!' Shari was relieved and yet . . . something else . . . something that niggled at her, but she couldn't put a finger on it. She only knew that, whatever it was, it had taken the shine off the day.

CHAPTER FOUR

IT was a shock to Shari, the following morning, to find that Griff had gone away. Annoyance faded into a kind of depression as she supposed it had probably never occurred to him to inform *her* of his plans. Estelle would have known, of course, and probably, as his hostess, her grandmother too. She should have been pleased to get rid of one of the 'off-comers' for a day or two, but it would have been better if it had been Estelle who had left. Shari certainly wasn't going to ask *her* where Griff was. Perhaps her grandmother? Later, when they were alone.

But it was Abigail Freeman's day for going to the hospital. Since her series of strokes she had been attending a clinic at regular intervals for routine checks, and immediately after breakfast, Lily came in to say that Abigail's taxi had arrived.

Feeling uncharacteristically at a loss, Shari wandered out to the stables and while she mucked out Rainbow's stall, she brooded on the inconsiderate, secretive behaviour of *some people*. But vigorous exercise she'd found always had the effect of banishing depression, and before long her spirits had risen and she was asking herself scornfully why it should matter two hoots to her what Griff Masterson did.

Her chore finished, she went along to the farm office, where she found Jimmy, his head, as usual, bent over mounds of paperwork.

'Well this is a surprise. To what do I owe this honour? What have I done to deserve a visit from you?'

Taken aback, Shari tried to laugh off the remark. He was joking of course.

'Am I interrupting something important? I always visit you in the office, and you've never . . .'

'Not lately, you haven't!' Jimmy pointed out with a teasing smile. 'You've been rather busy lately, gallivanting about with Griff Masterson.'

'We haven't been "gallivanting",' she told him indignantly, 'it's been business, to do with Threlkeld's future.'

'Oh yes, and since when have *you* been so anxious to co-operate with the new owners?' Jimmy asked insinuatively. 'I don't see you spending as much time with Estelle as you do with Griff.'

'Naturally not!' She was beginning to feel uncomfortable. 'You know very well I only agreed to work here on condition that I didn't have to take orders from *her*. The same applies to you, you're responsible to Griff too.'

'I've no objection to working for Estelle,' Jimmy said, surprisingly. 'She's got a good head on her shoulders. Personally I think you're too hard on her.'

While Shari gaped, he bent his head once more over his ledgers. She longed to persuade him that *her* view of Estelle's character was the correct one. She also wanted to refute his insinuations about herself and Griff, yet to do so would make them assume too much importance. She knew the dangers of protesting too much. She fidgeted about the office.

'For goodness sake, Shari!' Jimmy said at last. 'Haven't you got anything useful to do?'

'No,' she said forlornly, 'and I don't want to hang around the house. There's only *her* there this morning. Gran's at the hospital and . . .'

'And Griff's away, and so you don't know what to do with yourself. Hasn't it struck you as rather odd, Shar? Once upon a time the days never seemed long enough for you, and now, here you are, bored, and it's not even ten o'clock.'

'It . . . it must be the thought of all the changes,' she said hastily. 'None of the usual things seem worth doing somehow, because I'm not doing them for *us*, but for *them*.'

Jimmy threw down his pen, giving her all his attention, since it was obvious he wasn't going to be allowed to work in peace.

'Are you *sure* that's all it is?' he asked.

'Yes, nothing's just for me and Gran any more. Threlkeld won't belong to us soon.'

'I see.' He studied her face consideringly. He dared not give voice to his thoughts. If he was right, she would know soon enough. Just lately Shari's moods had been more volatile than usual, a fact which only served to confirm his theory.

'Of course I know it must seem like losing your home too,' she said, thinking she had wounded his feelings because he had been silent for so long.

'Never mind the farm, or the Hall, but what about Griff Masterson?' he asked.

'I thought you *liked* him?' she puzzled. 'It's Estelle that's the trouble. She's the one who wants to buy.'

'Oh, Shari!' Jimmy sounded amused, but exasperated too. 'I love this place, of course I do. But I'm realistic about it. Threlkeld's not the only place in the world. Someday I want a place of my own, a family. And that's what *you* should be thinking about, you're not getting any younger,' he pointed out with the easy frankness of long acquaintance.

'Thank you very much! So I'm probably all set to be an old maid? I don't care! I've never seen a man yet who could make me want to leave Beckdale.'

'What about Griff?' he murmured casually, studying her reactions carefully.

Shari looked at him in total astonishment.

'Griff? Don't be ridiculous, he's going to marry Estelle, and anyway . . .'

'Is he?' Jimmy interrupted. 'Where's her ring then?

Have you heard any talk of marriage plans?'

'No, but that's their business, surely. You don't think,' her tone was shocked, 'that they just plan to *live* together?'

'Would that matter?' he said casually, then, as she remained totally still, obviously struck dumb by the thought he had placed in her mind, 'Look, I've got to work. Since you apparently haven't, how about starting Rainbow's training for the Show?' He meant the Agricultural Show, in August, at which there were riding events.

'I hadn't thought of entering this year,' she said vaguely, her mind still on his shocking suggestion.

'Why ever not? You always have.'

'It's different this year. It won't be for Threlkeld.'

'No, damn it!' He was near to exasperation again. 'But it'll be for *you*. Haven't we just been talking about this very thing? That there's more to life than Threlkeld? The house could burn down tomorrow and then where would you be? Do it for yourself, for Mrs Freeman. You know how proud she's always been of your riding, because you take after your grandfather.' Shari's father hadn't been interested in horses. 'I thought you had more character than that, to let your whole life wither and collapse just because . . .'

'I have, I *have*!' Stung to retort, she made for the door. 'All right, I suppose it might be fun at that. But I'll have to go and inspect the jumps first. They may need some repairs.'

'I had one of the men look them over and repaint them the other day,' Jimmy said, 'but as *you* haven't been near the little paddock lately . . .'

'Oh, Jimmy!' Violet eyes sparkled and impetuously she flew at him to give him a hug. 'I don't know what I'd do without you.' She turned on her heel; her mood had undergone a lightning change; she was now all eagerness to begin.

She didn't hear Jimmy's muttered words.

'You'll manage without me all right, but somehow and I'm afraid you're not going to get him, I don't think you'll manage without Griff, you poor kid!' It was some time before he returned his attention to the farm accounts.

The jumping course in the paddock was set out in a very professional style and Rainbow appeared to have caught some of Shari's enthusiasm.

'If you keep this up,' she told the mare, patting her neck, 'we shan't disgrace ourselves in August.'

Making her way back towards the stable, she encountered Estelle. Surprised, for the other woman rarely ventured beyond house and garden, Shari gave her a cool yet civil greeting. But it soon became apparent that Estelle had come in search of her and she wasted no time in coming to the point of her errand.

'Shari, we have to talk and while Griff is away seems as good a time as any. When he's here there never seems to be any opportunity. Look, can't you make an effort to be polite at least? It would make things more comfortable all round, especially as I've asked your grandmother if Griff and I can stay on as her paying guests indefinitely. You see, we might decide to buy more than just one property and this is a good base to work from.'

'If you're going to buy other places,' Shari returned, 'why bother with Threlkeld at all?'

'If it hadn't been me,' Estelle said sharply, 'someone else would have bought the house. Why do you dislike me so much? Can't you give me a frank answer?'

Estelle, Shari thought, would probably like her to be rude again, giving her an excuse to have Griff dismiss her after all. So she tried to answer calmly.

'Dislike you? I've barely given you a thought.'

'Oh, come now, Shari. That isn't true and you know

it. Surely it's not just because you won't be "lady of the manor" any more. You couldn't be that childish, surely?'

'Threlkeld isn't a Manor House actually.' Shari couldn't resist the sting in the tail. 'So I'm afraid *you* won't be "lady of the manor" either.' Beneath the perfection of her make-up, which must have taken hours to achieve, Shari observed with guilty satisfaction that Estelle had flushed. Her shot had gone home. Nevertheless, the other woman persevered.

'Shari, believe me. I do understand your feelings. But whether you approve or not, I may well be mistress here some day and I'm sorry, but I'm just not prepared to put up with any more insolence. Griff may have agreed to accept responsibility for your good behaviour, but he won't turn a blind eye on deliberate rudeness either.' She glanced at Rainbow. 'And once we do take over here, there'll be no "playing at horses". You'll be expected to earn your keep.'

'Really?' Shari enquired innocently. 'But that's exactly what I will be doing, not "playing" but looking after *Griff's* horses.'

Despite her poise, Estelle was showing distinct signs of frustration at her inability to reason with Shari and she took out her frustration in what seemed to be the only sure way of disturbing the younger girl.

'Don't be too sure of that!' she snapped. 'The property, the house, the outbuildings *and* the land will be mine. I might just decide to veto this scheme of Griff's. Horrible creatures, horses!' She shuddered. Her words were retaliatory but there was no doubt of her very real distaste. She might indeed be glad of a reason for banning Griff's animals.

'It sounds,' Shari said innocently, 'as if you intend to "wear the trousers". Do you think Griff is the type of man to stand for that?'

'I think I know considerably more about Griff than

you do,' Estelle said quietly, 'and one thing I do know is that he's very loyal to his friends and we've been friends for years. Don't imagine, just because he takes a fatherly interest in you . . .'

'Goodness!' Shari exclaimed in apparent wonder. 'Are you and Griff really *that* old?'

'Griff has interceded for you in the past, Shari. But don't feel too secure. If I do decide to buy, in the final analysis I'll have the last word about who's employed here. I think you're being very foolish. You're cutting off your nose to spite your face.'

And to herself, Shari admitted ruefully that the other woman's remark was justified. But somehow, where Estelle was concerned, she seemed unable to restrain a hostility which seemed to increase, in spite of her recognition that Griff was a very likeable man, who would probably fit in very well with the valley folk.

'I understand you've been giving Rainbow a work out.' Abigail Freeman said to her granddaughter over lunch. 'Did she go well for you?'

'Splendidly!' Shari said enthusiastically.

'Good. I always look forward to the Show, to seeing a Freeman in the jumping arena.' Abigail sighed wistfully and her gaze went, as it often did, to the oil-painting above the fireplace, which showed her late husband, mounted on a fine chestnut.

'When do you expect Mr Masterson back?' Abigail asked Estelle presently. Shari waited tensely for the reply.

'I can't really say. He said he had several things to attend to. He has a partnership in a firm of solicitors in the city; and I believe he intends to visit his parents while he's away. They live in Herefordshire, you know. In fact they're our nearest neighbours. Griff and I grew up together. His family is one of the best in the county.'

Shari rarely exchanged meal-time conversation with

Estelle, but her imp of mischief could not overlook what she saw as pretentiousness on the other woman's part. It was just too good an opportunity to miss.

'I've often wondered,' she said in a tone of innocent enquiry, 'just what people mean by "one of the best families"? Does it mean they're renowned for their good works?'

'Oh, Shari!' Mrs Freeman laughed indulgently at her granddaughter's professed ignorance, but Estelle replied somewhat sharply.

'Don't be ridiculous. You must know it refers to their breeding. They're distantly related to royalty; and Griff's uncle is Lord Geoffrey Masterson.'

'Oh, I don't go in for snobbery,' Shari said airily. But this piece of information was enough to keep her musing quietly throughout the rest of the meal. Had Lord Geoffrey any children? Or could Griff be in line, eventually, for a title? Estelle, she imagined, would greatly enjoy being Lady Masterson. Immersed in thought, she was still aware of Estelle explaining that Griff didn't *need* to work, that he would much rather have helped to run his father's estate, but that was incumbent upon his elder brother.

'At heart he's not really the office type. He'd much prefer the outdoor life, hence his keenness to go in with me and my project.'

The weeks passed. To Shari they seemed long and uneventful; but she took care never to appear idle, to give Jimmy cause to tease her about being at a loss without Griff. But it was surprising how much she did miss his presence around the place; the sight of him crossing the yard, with those long, athletic strides of his; the sound of his deep voice in conversation. At mealtimes, she found herself strangely conscious of his empty chair.

One of the tasks she set herself, apart from caring for and training Rainbow, was that of cleaning out and refurbishing the rest of the stable block, so that it would be ready for the ponies Griff intended to purchase. Structurally they had been well maintained, but there was a litter of old straw, cobwebs had festooned every corner and hung from the mangers. And a fresh coat of paint on the outside wouldn't come amiss.

She was employed on the painting one warm May afternoon when she heard the sound of a car approaching the front of the house. Surveying her paint-bedaubed hands and clothes, she hoped her grandmother wasn't expecting visitors.

At the sound of footsteps ringing on the cobbled yard, she swung round and, a totally unexpected reaction, felt her heart leap with joyful recognition. Unthinkingly, she dropped her paintbrush and impetuously she flew across the yard, stopping short only of throwing herself, paint stains and all, into the arms of the immaculately suited man.

'Griff! Griff! You're *back*!' Her greeting was warm, spontaneous and totally unselfconscious, as she looked up at him, violet eyes sparkling with pleasure, the smile that somehow only his presence seemed to evoke these days irradiating her oval face.

Apparently untroubled by her disreputable appearance or the inevitable damage to his impeccable grey suit, he swung her off her feet, his arms holding her hard against his chest, his mouth seeking hers in a kiss, a kiss that it never occurred to her to evade, so natural did it seem. But a few seconds later, she realised, bemusedly, that he had not kissed her *this* way before; he had been gentle with her, lightly affectionate; but now his lips parted hers in a blazing, consuming demand, that seemed to plumb her to the depths of all the mixed emotions she felt at his return, his tongue, moist, warm and pleasant-tasting, stroking, tantalising her mouth's soft inner lining.

With delight, she recognised the familiar scent of

him, the freshness of aftershave, the scent of his skin,
which seemed to be uniquely his. No other man had
pleased her sensitive nostrils so. She felt *right* in his
arms, safe. Now that he was back everything would be
all right, she needn't fear Estelle's threats. Griff would
protect her.

Without relaxing the fierceness of his grip, he let her
slide down over the sinewy strength of his hard,
masculine presence. She could feel the muscles of his
thighs, firm, unyielding. With no prior warning, with no
expectation of what was to come, she felt a terrible,
dagger-like pain shaft through her body. Fear gripped
her. What was the matter with her? She felt far more
breathless than her impetuous rush across the stable
yard warranted and in short, nervous gasps, she tried to
ease the sudden constriction in her breast. Lost,
bewildered by a totally unfamiliar sensation, she looked
up into sapphire-blue eyes, seemed to drown in their
darkened depths. A small cloud of anxiety began to
form, blurring the edges of her mind. Something,
somewhere was wrong, troubling her.

'Have you missed me then, Shari?' It was a perfectly
reasonable question, in view of her enthusiastic
greeting, but the cloud beginning to engulf her spirits
grew larger and blacker.

Her throat seemed to close up, so that she could not
answer him. Was that why life at Threlkeld had suddenly
seemed so flat and purposeless, in vain? Not for the
reasons she'd given Jimmy? Not because of Estelle's
threatening presence, but because of *Griff's* absence?

The nerves in the lower part of her body still seemed
to be fluttering madly. Unknown to her the budding
of sexual awareness, a new, hitherto unexperienced
craving, his unexpected return had brought to life.

He repeated his question, his tone tenderly amused by
her obvious confusion.

Yes, she'd missed him. But until this moment she

hadn't realised just why. And the knowledge frightened her. Something within her cried out in regret for the lost days of her youth and innocence, days of unruffled peace of mind, that could never come again. She felt exposed, as if her emotion must be naked to that shrewd sapphire stare and she fought an inward, desperate battle. But it was no good. She knew now that the almost unendurable joy she had felt on seeing him, the pain that her body experienced in his arms, were the pangs of love, and that long, sensuous kiss, the brush of his hard body against hers as he'd set her down, had taught her so much.

Dear God, she had never suspected that physical proximity to a man could make you ache so. Yet now that she looked back, hadn't this new sensation been growing steadily, from the very first time she had innocently received kisses, that *she* had believed to be as innocently bestowed, a token of forgiveness, of friendship? Looking back, she knew that the strange warning she had experienced then had been the mere budding of sexual desire. Somehow Griff's absence had acted as a catalyst, and his return had brought about the full flowering of awareness.

This was love, the emotion that until now she had always despised, had not understood in others. It had taken her a long time to come to the knowledge of her femininity and its needs; but now she had, and she had the painful sensation of something being physically torn from her. Chill tremors scudded down her spine and she felt the cold, sour taste of nausea. If this was love, then she didn't want it. It hurt. It was no good loving someone who didn't love you! And Griff belonged to Estelle. She recalled the other woman's words, 'He takes a *fatherly* interest in you.'

This, his most recent kiss, hadn't *seemed* fatherly. Perhaps he did find her attractive. But that was impossible. She was no eye-catching beauty, and look at her now, in her scruffiest jeans and shirt, smothered in paint. She knew there was even paint on her face, in her hair. How *could* he find anything in her to make him want to kiss her as a woman, rather than as a child? She could not help the small sob that escaped her.

'Shari? What is it?' His voice was concerned now. 'I thought you were pleased to see me, but you seem to have turned into a block of stone, and why are you crying? Is something wrong?'

'No, of course not!' She wrenched herself free of him, dashing a paint-stained hand across her eyes. 'I'm just overtired, I expect. I think I'll go and clean up and have a rest.'

Backing away from him, a movement caught her eye and she saw Estelle standing only a few yards away. Of course, *she* had come out to greet Griff, as was her right, and she must have seen everything! With a choking cry, Shari turned and fled for Rainbow's stall, the only sanctuary that offered, since to reach the house she would have had to pass Estelle, to run the gauntlet of an accusing stare, perhaps even a remark about her impulsive behaviour.

Snatching up a dandy brush, she began to work on Rainbow's already gleaming flanks, grooming automatically, her mind going over and over the revelations of the last ten minutes in a nightmarish, unbroken circle. So far as she could see, and she could not see one hour beyond the devastating present, this was the end of happiness for her.

She hadn't *meant* to fall in love, not for years and years. Love meant a surrender of individuality and she didn't want her happiness, her peace of mind to depend upon somebody else. She felt an almost unbearable nostalgia for the past, even the very recent past when at least, even with her worries over Threlkeld, she had been heart-whole and carefree.

Although she knew she was indulging in self-torture,

she let her mind dwell on the few previous occasions when Griff had kissed her. *Then* she had only *sensed* danger. If only she had realised its nature, she might have been able to draw back in time, to spin a protective cocoon of distrust about her heart, for how could you trust a man who made love to one woman, when he was shortly to marry another?

She couldn't live on memories alone yet she found herself dwelling on those early, tentative, tender kisses, which had not lasted long, but which must have played their part in her gradual awakening. Today, she thought wonderingly, he had kissed her *as a woman*. Had he known? Had he recognised the difference, the change in her? The heat of humiliation engulfed her whole body. Don't let him have guessed, she breathed inwardly, that would be the most dreadful thing of all, to have him pity her.

Feverishly, her mind darted in another direction. If he *hadn't* guessed, perhaps it wasn't too late, perhaps there was still time to adopt an attitude of cool indifference towards him, to treat him to the same hostility she accorded Estelle?

She had to reason this out; but the waves of feeling that still swamped her were making coherent thought impossible. She was too close to events here, too close to *him*. She had to get away. With nervous fingers that trembled and fumbled, she saddled and bridled her pony, terrified now that she would not be allowed time in which to make her escape. Not bothering with a jacket, but snatching her hard hat from a peg, she led Rainbow out on to the cobbles of the yard.

She did not relax until she was clear of the weathered grey farm buildings, making her way across the slanting fields towards the foothills.

The lovely green bowl that was the Beckdale Valley echoed to the noise of the sheep and their newly born lambs, little clumsy bundles of wool, white with black faces. There were a hundred new lambs belonging to Threlkeld this spring, most of them born while Griff had been away.

Lakeland had made its leap from spring into summer, the countryside radiant under the increasing warmth of the sun. It was a time of year for light spirits, for happiness, for love, and here was she, the most miserable unloved creature, at this moment, on God's earth. Tears rolled down her cheeks as she rode, blurring the view, turning the varied, luscious greens into a chaotic amalgam of colour.

It was not necessary to climb the dividing ridge to reach the valley of Ramsdale. One could ride there, following an old pack-horse trail, once the natural and only communication between one valley and another.

There had been rain overnight and the sunshine on the newly washed countryside seemed to bring out the bright colours of leaves and blossoms, the bluebell carpeting of the fells, the sparkle of silver in the crags. Even the starker ridges had a friendly, benevolent look as they lay, one behind the other, as far as the eye could see. Here and there a pool of rainwater or some lovely reed-edged tarn shimmered in the heat haze.

Gradually, but insistently, the beauties of nature forced themselves on Shari's attention, but could not bring their usual comfort. Angrily, she railed against a fate which had played her the one trick that could now separate her from her beloved dales. For she would have to go away. It would no longer be right, or bearable, to stay and work for Griff with so many opportunties of accidental contact. But she couldn't leave Threlkeld until her grandmother and Lily were safely settled in their cottage. She could only then think of her own future. In one way she was glad of an excuse to push the thought of that future to one side. It seemed such a bleak and empty prospect.

*   *.   *

Rainbow walked steadily on, coming now to a
footbridge over a beck, following the beck's downward
course to Ramsdale Tarn. They seemed to have reached
the Ramsdale Valley very quickly, Shari thought; too
quickly for her, still on her merry-go-round of
conflicting ideas. She did not consult her watch. She
just knew she was not ready to go home yet and she
pointed the pony's head at Scaldmoor, over which a
track ran to Blawdale. Two valleys away from home!
When she needed to put the whole world between
herself and Griff! The track over Scaldmoor was an old
corpse road, reputedly haunted by the spirit of a horse,
which had bolted when carrying its dead burden.
Though Shari was as imaginative as most, the old story
did not trouble her. She was haunted by her own
ghosts, looming large enough to obscure fears of any
spectral, mounted corpse.

So engrossed was she in her thoughts that she was
almost in Blawdale before she noted the change in the
weather. What had begun as a sunny day had
gradually become more and more oppressive, the kind
of stifling heat often followed by torrential downpours,
and sure enough large black clouds had massed,
obscuring the sun, casting their shadows on the
mountain tops, making them look grey and harsh. It
would be wise to turn back, little as she relished her
return home.

She turned Rainbow's head and made for home at a
steady trot. There was no mistaking the still, hushed
threat of the coming storm. Anxiously, she looked up
at the sky. How would her pony react to the elemental
violence? She'd never had Rainbow out in a storm
before.

The animal had scented the coming weather; her
actions had become excitable and nervous, her eyes
rolling back at Shari as if for reassurance. Shari urged
her to greater speed, but as they broke into a canter the

storm overtook them. Now almost the whole sky was an angry blue-black, the remainder a lurid orange.

At first rain fell in big, irregular drops on the dusty track, then turned to hailstones, lashing Shari's face and stinging the pony's flanks. Then it poured down steadily, swept this way and that by the driving wind that accompanied it. Shari was soon soaked through.

The weather did nothing to help her depression and she knew that, mingled with the rain that streamed down her cheeks, were her own despairing tears; tears at the predicament she was in and what she might have to face in the weeks to come.

It had taken only minutes for the fellsides to become alive with a hundred rivulets, becks were soon overflowing and surging in a creamy fury down the hillsides, their overspill crossing the horse's path. Somewhere up on the slopes there must have been a cloudburst.

Plunging skittishly across a slope covered with a streaming mud, the usually sure-footed Rainbow slipped and stumbled and Shari, not as alert as usual, took a toss just as a clap of thunder seemed to roll around the sky, like a gigantic roulette ball. Rainbow bolted.

Covered in sticky mud, bruised and winded, Shari stumbled to her feet, able only to stand and watch as her mount disappeared into the distance.

From start to finish the storm had lasted perhaps half an hour; but in all her life, Shari could not remember weather of such unsurpassed wildness. It was almost as if the elements had responded to and reflected her own turmoil.

With one of Lakeland's sudden, characteristic changes, the sun parted the clouds with a bright, watery sunshine. But the cessation of the storm brought the tired, wet girl no relief. She still had to make her way home, weary and despondent.

But why drag all the way home? The word no longer had any validity. No longer held its warm attraction. It was as if she had already conceded possession to Estelle. She was close to Charlie Garner's farm. Charlie and his wife would make a fuss of her, allow her to rest and dry out, and suddenly she needed to be cosseted, made much of.

Her reception at the Garners' farm was as she had anticipated and Elsie Garner insisted that she take a hot bath immediately.

'Of course Charlie will phone your Gran, love and put her mind at rest,' she said in answer to Shari's anxious request. 'They're bound to worry when Rainbow arrives home without you.'

Warm once more and clad in a pair of slacks and a sweater belonging to Elsie, she came down to find a large mug of soup awaiting her, together with a generous slice of warm home-made bread.

'*Did* Charlie phone?' she asked at once.

'Your pony's home safe and your Gran was relieved to hear you were all right. But the message about you got through too late to stop them sending out a search party. Jimmy and two of the men are out and that nice Mr Masterson. Wherever did you meet him, love? Is he *the one*? Somehow we always thought you and young Jimmy . . .'

Considering the efficiency of the local bush telegraph, Shari was surprised that Griff's identity and his business in Beckdale were not known to all and sundry, but the time had definitely come, she felt, to make his position clear.

'I'm surprised your niece hasn't been over to see you in all this time and explained,' she said to Elsie and to Charlie who had rejoined them, 'Griff Masterson is going into partnership with Estelle at Threlkeld. He's going to . . . to marry her.' She could not quite keep the tiny quiver out of her voice.

'Well, you *do* surprise me!' Charlie exclaimed.

'We'd heard she'd been over to Threlkeld, of course,' Charlie continued, 'staying on as a paying guest, isn't she, until she's looked the area over? Tell her to drop by sometime. We'll look forward to seeing her.'

'We're not exactly on those terms,' Shari said stiffly.

'Don't you like her, love?' Elsie asked. 'I know she can be a bit bossy; and I can't stand her mother, but Estelle's all right.'

'And you say that nice young fellow is going to marry her? Charlie still sounded incredulous. 'Are you sure you've got that right? Nay, lass, I could've sworn . . .' He looked thoughtfully at Shari's set little face. 'He seemed right fond of you.'

'Well, he isn't!' she snapped sharply out of her hurt, then realised her over-reaction was likely to cause more speculation, so she added a tense codicil. 'I'm just the hired help, kept on at my old home if I behave myself, because I know the area and because I'm good with horses.'

'Threlkeld's not actually sold yet though, is it?' Charlie asked.

'No, Estelle has to wait for the verdict from her financial advisers and no one's been near the place yet, to look it over.'

'Financial advisers, is it?' Charlie grinned. 'To think of our little Estelle with financial advisers. Muriel, that's her mother, moved in the best circles before she married our Sam. She asked one of her affluent friends to stand godmother to the child and when the godmother died a year since, what does the woman do but leave a colossal fortune to Estelle?'

'Lucky Estelle,' Shari said wryly.

'Aye,' Charlie said quietly, 'and she'll put the money to good use. She'll not fritter it.'

'Some people seem to have all the luck, don't they, Shari love?' Elsie said sympathetically. 'I'll bet you wish you could have some of that money, so you could keep your home. But Estelle seems to have been born with a silver spoon in her mouth. Things always did fall into her lap.'

And now she's got Griff as well, Shari thought painfully.

It was as though Griff had been put into her mind by some telepathic awareness.

'That young man's just coming up the path,' Charlie announced, 'the one you say is engaged to our Estelle and by the heck! He's got a black look about him!'

'Oh!' Shari felt herself begin to tremble. He wasn't even in the same room with her yet; just the knowledge of his approach had set her nerves twanging.

The heavy knocker on the front door rose and fell with impatient repetition, its hammer-blows only a little more violent than the beating of her heart.

'I'd best let him in before he breaks the door down,' Charlie muttered. 'He seems to be in an all-fired hurry.'

In a hurry to attack her. Fists clenched in her lap, Shari's mesmerised gaze remained fixed on the door through which Griff must soon appear. She heard the opening words of Charlie's casual, friendly greeting cut short by the terse demand,

'All right! Where is she?'

She heard the ring of booted feet on the flagged passageway. He had to duck his head in order to clear the lintel, but once inside the room, he drew himself up to his full height.

She'd never seen Griff angry before. She'd been rude and hostile to him in the early days of his arrival at Threlkeld, but throughout he had remained calm and reasonable. Why *should* he be angry now? Today's misfortune had involved only herself. She supposed he might have been inconvenienced by the necessity of searching for her. But it wasn't *her* fault that the searchers had set out so precipitately, before the message that she was safe got through.

'So *there* you are! Safe, warm and comfortable, while everyone else is thrown into a turmoil by your escapade.'

'She wasn't warm and comfortable when she arrived here,' Elsie put in placatingly.

'Serves her right then! Wilful, petulant little termagant!' He addressed Shari. 'Do you *ever* think before you act?'

'I don't know what you mean,' she said spiritedly. It was easier to face him than she'd feared, easier because he was angry with her and not his usual easy-going self, which might have disarmed her, weakened her. 'I can't see anything wrong in going for a ride.'

'Not properly prepared, no, and with an eye to the weather. You aspire to be so knowledgeable about your countryside, so you should know the signs of an imminent storm, But off you go, hell for leather, with no coat on, and you obviously rode too far, just like the sulky child you still are.'

'Sulky? Child?' Shari was so enraged that she could hardly repeat the offensive words.

'Yes, childish! That's how your behaviour strikes me. This ridiculous feud you've got going with Estelle, and for no reason. I've heard something of what went on between you while I've been away.'

Estelle's version, of course. What lies had the other woman woven in among the true facts of their disagreements?

'And,' Griff continued, 'I thought for a moment that you were really pleased to see me. But you're just as prejudiced against both of us as ever, aren't you?'

That 'us' struck a cold chill in her blood: 'him and Estelle.'

'I *was* pleased to see you,' she began feebly.

'So much so that you didn't bother to wait.'

'Estelle,' she began, not knowing how to put into words her concern that the other woman had seen her in Griff's arms.

'Estelle!' he repeated. 'Yes, that's it. You assumed, jumped to conclusions as usual.'

She honestly didn't know what he was talking about, but stared at him, violet eyes wide with distress, mouth beginning to quiver painfully.

'Would you like us to leave you alone?' Charlie began tactfully. 'To talk over whatever it is you . . .'

'No!' Griff snapped. Then, remembering that it was his host to whom he spoke, 'Thank you, no! I've come to take this spoilt brat home. I'll deal with her as she deserves there!'

'Then deal easily with her, young man,' Charlie said sharply. 'She's suffered enough today already.'

'And have *you* the right to deal with her?' Elsie put in.

'Maybe not,' Griff admitted, 'but it's time someone did. Have you any idea of what Mrs Freeman went through? When one of the men reported that pony coming back to its stable, riderless, in such weather? You'll hardly claim that Shari's grandmother is up to dealing with her as forcibly as she deserves.' Then, to Shari, 'Come on, I've got the car outside, and a hundred jobs waiting for me back at Threlkeld.'

'Shari,' Charlie said firmly, 'you don't have to go with Mr Masterson, unless you want to. I'll run you home myself.'

For an instant Shari considered taking him at his word, but then she shook her head. That Griff was determined on some sort of confrontation was pretty obvious. Repudiating his company would only postpone it. 'I'm not afraid of Mr Masterson's threat. Whatever he says, he has no jurisdiction over me. He and Miss Garner don't own Threlkeld yet.'

'I'm beginning to think it'll be a damned shame if

they do!' Charlie returned almost savagely. He looked at Griff's implacable expression. 'Seems to me I've revised my opinion of you! Shari here means a lot to me, Masterson. If I hear you've been treating her unfairly or unkindly, you'll have me to deal with. Aye, and what's more there'll be no ponies changing hands between Ramsdale and Beckdale neither.'

Griff made no reply, merely waited imperiously for Shari to precede him out to the car.

As he ushered her into the passenger seat, his hand accidentally brushed hers and she had a wild impulse to leap out again, to say she'd changed her mind, that she wanted Charlie to see her home after all. It wasn't that she was really afraid of Griff's anger. It was the thought of their proximity in the car, for the time it would take them to negotiate the long, tortuous road from Ramsdale to Beckdale; and she wedged herself as tightly against the door and as far away from Griff as she could.

'I'll send your riding things over when they're cleaned and dry,' Elsie called. 'Sure you'll be all right, love?'

Shari made an attempt at a reassuring smile, but as the powerful car pulled away from the Garner farmhouse, she felt far from certain that she *would* be 'all right'.

CHAPTER FIVE

AFTER the storm, it was a beautiful evening; the sun, as if to make up for its earlier defection, was making the most of its second departure and the mountains too borrowed the colours of the western sky, turning grey buildings to pink and lilac.

'This isn't the way home,' she ventured. Griff had not spoken one word to her since he'd taken his place in the car and the long silence had become strained, like the uneasy calm that had preceded the afternoon's storm.

'No,' he agreed shortly.

'Where are we going?' she asked with a little more insistence.

'Nowhere in particular!'

'What about the hundred jobs you had waiting?'

'Never mind that.' Then, as she could not restrain a small, exasperated sigh, '*I just need to think!* So be quiet, will you!'

Shari was beginning to feel decidedly ruffled and not at all inclined to comply with this peremptory order. But there was something in the mood of the man beside her, some tangible aura emanating from him that made her reluctant to cross him. She did not recognise Griff in this mood and somehow the unknown was frightening.

The car was not moving very fast. Griff drove not dangerously, but certainly as one abstracted, more concerned with his thoughts than with the mechanics of his task. They came at last to the great sheet of water that was Thirlmere, the road playing hide-and-seek with the lake, passing through plantations of conifers. At last, when Shari wondered if he was intending to drive on indefinitely in this aimless manner, Griff slowed and pulled the car into a quiet spot, overlooking the lake. He switched off the ignition and leant back in his seat; but there was no sense of relaxation in him and now that he was no longer driving, his tension communicated itself to Shari. She knew somehow that *this* was the moment of reckoning.

She stared straight ahead of her, aware that he had turned to look at her and unwilling to meet the keen penetration of his eyes.

'What am I to do with you, Shari Freeman?' His tone was still curt, exasperated.

'It depends just what you *mean* by that,' she retorted, her eyes still on the panorama of lake, mountain and sky. 'Surely,' sarcastically, 'you'll need to consult Estelle about a suitable penance, as you did last time.'

'Right at this moment,' he said and sounded savage, his voice oddly unlike its usual smooth, deep tones, 'the only thing I feel like consulting is my instinct and my instinct tells me to put you across my knee and teach you a lesson you won't forget in a hurry.'

If the light had been better, Shari knew that her face would be seen to have paled. He wouldn't? He wouldn't *dare*. She told him so, but her only response was a mirthless laugh.

'Don't you dare me to do anything! There's nothing of which I don't feel capable right at this moment, including strangulation!'

Now he *was* exaggerating. Now she *knew* he couldn't possibly mean what he said. It was too extreme and Shari's tension evaporated in high, nervous laughter.

'Don't laugh at me, damn you!'

His reaction was so swift that she could not possibly have anticipated it, much less prevented it, and the laughter died in her throat as he grabbed her, dragging her unceremoniously into his arms, her body tightly constrained between the hardness of his chest and the uncomfortable arc of the steering wheel, so that resistance was impossible. Then his mouth descended upon hers in a savage, grinding possession which bruised her lips, bringing tears of pain to her eyes, though she vowed that he would not elicit one cry from her.

As he swung her upright once more, she concluded that his anger had expended itself, that now she might vent her own outrage at this cavalier treatment; but she was wrong. He did not release her, she was still imprisoned in the steely circle of his arms, his sinewy strength easily stemming all her attempts at evasion. She had laughed before at the idea that he might harm her, but now she felt a stir of something which was definitely not amusement, now that she understood her own reactions to him for what they were. Close to like this, in the intimacy of his car, Griff had a sensuality that set her pulses racing, pulses that she strove to subdue. But this was not the Griff *she* knew, gentle, teasingly tender. He kissed her again, savagely, punishingly, inflicting more bruises on her soft lips. There was not a flicker of tenderness in his kiss.

Again she tried to fight him off, tried to steel herself against the effect of his kisses, which, in spite of the pain they inflicted, were threatening to sweep away her resistance.

But the hunting, hurting kiss continued, not a caress but an abrasion. Yet despite his misuse of her, she felt a deep-seated, peculiar pulsing of excitement. She had fallen in love with Griff, with his gentle tenderness, his equable nature, and yet this was a different side to him, equally compelling, a wild, primeval magnetism, which awoke a similar response in her. She had never thought of love as being a fierce, demanding passion, as capable of violence as of sweetness, but now she could feel it in her veins, in her blood.

She felt herself giving in to the tide of sensuousness which was sweeping through her and her secret hunger made her respond with all the fervour of which she was capable. At that moment she was not conscious of right or wrong; she only knew that her body clamoured to be close to his.

When he thrust her away violently, she was so unprepared for his action that she fell against the door.

'That,' he said in a strangled tone, 'was for risking your bloody, stupid little neck and scaring the living daylights out of me. How,' he asked, still in that tortured voice, 'how do you think it felt, riding over that old corpse road, expecting that at any moment I might find a real one, *yours*?'

'I . . . I . . .' she stammered, but she was allowed to go no further, as he pulled her back into his arms, this time showering small soft kisses over her eyelids, her cheeks, her neck and finally her mouth, a languorous process that sent fresh tremors through her. His mouth was warm and gentle now, as she remembered it, coaxing, its sensuality tender rather than provocative.

'And *that*,' he said, in a brief interval between kisses, 'is because I'm so glad I *didn't* find what I feared . . . that you're safe.'

She pulled a little away from him, though he refused to release her totally.

'But *why*?' she said, puzzled. 'Why were you so angry? When I was perfectly all right?'

He gave a sigh, half exasperation, half amusement; all the tension had gone out of him; he was his usual self now and he pulled her head down against his shoulder as he spoke, his eyes unseeingly on the expanse of water before them.

'Haven't you ever seen a small child run into the path of an oncoming vehicle? Haven't you seen its mother's reaction? The child escapes death by a hairsbreadth, the mother should be rejoicing and yet in all probability, that child gets his legs severely slapped and a savage tongue-lashing to boot. It seems to be a natural reaction to stress . . . this violent anger, the need to punish.'

'Since when have *you* been *my* parent?'

'Believe me, Shari,' there was conviction in his voice, 'there is nothing remotely fatherly in the way I feel towards you just now.'

Confidently, she waited for him to kiss her again, certain that it would be a different experience yet again; but to her disappointment, he made no move to do so.

From where she sat, head closely against him, she could just see the dashboard clock and with amazement realised that scarcely twenty minutes had elapsed since Griff had parked the car, twenty minutes in which she had run the gamut of a hundred emotions. In that time the great sheet of water before them had lost all its daytime colour, turning from blue to metallic silver, against which once white swans had become mere silhouettes, leaving in their wake silvery lines. Imperceptibly, moving from light to half light, night had come, Lakeland was asleep.

So was she, nearly, she realised, exhausted by the intensity of the day's experiences, by her pendulum swings of emotion, lulled by the comfort and warmth of Griff's body; and yet she didn't want to sleep, didn't want to miss one of these precious moments. Half hoping that the movement would induce him to kiss her again, she turned her face up to look at his profile, an impenetrable mask against the night sky.

'*Griff?*' she questioned.

He seemed to come to himself with a start, as though his thoughts had been light years away, not with her. Where then? With whom? Estelle? She felt the hot thrust of jealousy, a sensation followed by the heat of shame. How *could* she have allowed him to treat her so?

She hadn't the physical strength to resist, but belatedly awakened pride told her she should have tried harder.

'Time I took you home!' Firmly, impersonally, he

restored her to her own half of the seat and reached for the ignition key.

On an instant mortified pride became white-hot fury. How could he kiss her like that, then just put her aside?

'Is that all you can say?' she demanded.

'What more do you want me to say?'

'Say!' Her voice came out, high, emotional, a revelation of her physical dissatisfaction. 'How about apologising to me for your abominable behaviour?'

'*My* behaviour!' He sounded amused and the engine purred into life. 'I thought the topic of the evening was *your* behaviour, for which you've now been suitably chastised.' His manner had reverted to its usual dismissal of her as a child.

The mood of desolation Shari experienced was beyond tears and yet her throat ached with their unshed burden. As far as he was concerned, this incident was over, to him just a method of inflicting punishment; but he had left her emotionally high and dry, an inner mass of contradictory conflict. Yet it was not in her nature to be cast down for long and piercing pride returned to help her, activating furious, blind rage.

How *dared* he take it upon himself to punish her again and in such a fashion? Punishment indeed! It had just been an outlet for his own basic instincts. He needn't think she was going to stay on meekly at Threlkeld once the property had changed hands. Her former resolve renewed itself; she would see her grandmother settled and then be on her way ... to where? She didn't know at the moment, but she would begin her investigations tomorrow as to how she could find a job, away from here, away from Griff.

Abigail Freeman was already in bed when they arrived home and Shari presented herself in her grandmother's room, to reassure her that she had suffered no injury, before going to bed herself.

'You're still as wild as ever!' Abigail sighed. 'But it's

not like you to be quite so reckless. What possessed you?'

Shari remained silent. Even to her grandmother she couldn't describe the cataclysm that had jolted the very foundations of her being.

'We were so worried,' Abigail continued. 'Mr Masterson did his best to reassure me, but I could see even he was almost beside himself with anxiety.' She sighed. 'Such a thoroughly *nice* man. If only he were buying Threlkeld on his own account, I'd feel so much easier. I've tried so hard but I can't like the idea of her . . . taking *my* place.'

'No one could ever do that,' Shari said affectionately, 'and *your* place will be wherever *you* are. It's not places that matter, but people,' she concluded slowly, wonderingly; when had she realised *that*?

'Oh!' Tears sprang into her grandmother's eyes. 'I'm so glad to hear you say that. I was afraid you'd never forgive me for selling Threlkeld. Under different circumstances, it would have been yours.'

About to prepare for bed, Shari, whose room overlooked the stableyard, heard an unusually loud clattering of hooves, a shrill whinny. Rainbow! The pony had arrived home safely, but there must have been something wrong with her after all. She snatched up a flashlight and sped downstairs, through the kitchen, the quickest route, unbolting the heavy old door with impatient fingers.

But she never reached Rainbow's box. The disturbance didn't come from there, and Rainbow's stall was not the only one occupied. Three other heads looked out over the half-doors and it was from one of these that the restless whinnying, the stamping hooves had sounded. Shari stopped short, seized with admiration. What a magnificent creature, a large chestnut, at least seventeen hands and strongly built by the look of his shoulders, all that her flashlight revealed.

Cautiously she held out a tentative hand, palm upwards, and the horse responded, snuffling eagerly, seeking for a titbit.

'Sorry, old boy. I've nothing to give you, but I will have in the morning.' She reached up and ran a hand over the smooth, muscular neck, feeling with pleasure its satiny texture.

Almost reluctantly, she moved on to inspect the occupants of the next two boxes. First a dainty mare so black that, had it not been for the white blaze on her nose, she would have been invisible against the shadowy interior of the loose box. A fine-boned creature, that Shari positively yearned to ride.

The resident in the third box was something totally different, quite outside Shari's experience. In some ways he resembled a draught horse, but he was smaller and lighter than a Shire, exceptionally attractive with his chestnut body and flaxen mane.

'That's Rusty!'

Shari nearly jumped out of her skin. Soft-footed, Griff had come up behind her and now he leant companionably beside her, shoulder brushing hers, the horse's head turning to him in a delighted whicker of recognition.

'He's beautiful,' she said, trying by her enthusiasm to conceal more troublesome responses to Griff himself. 'They're all beautiful, all three of them. When did they arrive?'

'This afternoon, with me,' he said wryly, 'only you didn't give me an opportunity to introduce you to them, or to thank you for preparing their new homes.'

'I didn't know you'd be bringing any horses. I was thinking of the fell ponies.'

'I don't think those tough little fillies will require such refinements, but *these* will and the others I hope to acquire, in time. Your grandmother kindly gave me permission to bring these animals with me, to stable them here until such time as the deal goes through.' A hand tucked through her arm, he led her back to the hunter's stall. 'This is Conker. He's getting on a bit, but he's still an impeccable jumper. And this,' leading her to the filly's box, 'is Jet. She's a lady's horse, not up to my weight.'

A lady's mount! Estelle disliked horses! So who would be riding Jet? Forgetting for a moment the necessity of leaving Threlkeld because there was no future for her with Griff, a little quiver of hope ran through Shari, that he mistook for a shiver.

'Cold?' he asked solicitously, putting his arm about her shoulders. 'What brought you out here without a coat?'

'I heard a horse complaining,' she explained, trying to ignore the effect that arm was having upon her heartbeats. 'I thought there was something wrong with Rainbow, but it was your hunter.'

'Mmmn. It'll be the strange surroundings. I'd just come out to look in on him myself. But he'll settle, He's a steady old fellow.'

'What sort of horse *is* Rusty?' she asked, moving back to the third stall, hoping that by so doing she would escape the disturbing confinement of that arm. But he moved with her, the grasp of his fingers tightening a little to prevent her eluding him.

'He's mostly Haflinger. They're an Austrian breed. My uncle owns several and he let me buy this chap from him because he's not pure bred. His mother somehow managed to break out of her paddock and committed an indiscretion with a neighbour's stallion. But he'll do for what I have in mind.' He sounded excited, she thought.

'Which is?'

'To cross-breed him with fell ponies. Haflingers are enormously good tempered, ideal for riding, especially for youngsters. There's a dash of Arab in them and they're a hardy mountain strain. In their native area, the South Tyrol, they manage on small rations and they don't need too much good grass or hard food; and even though Rusty's a half breed, he seems to have inherited more of his mother's characteristics than those of his sire. But let's get you back inside, you're still shivering; and you'll be able to get a better look at all three in the morning.'

Griff insisted that Shari have a hot drink.

'Yes, perhaps that is a good idea. I'll make one and take it up to my room.'

'I was hoping,' he said reproachfully, 'that I might be invited to join you.'

For one wild, terrifying moment she thought he meant in her room, and she felt her face flush scarlet. Then common sense prevailed and she realised that he expected to be offered a drink.

Seated on the opposite side of the kitchen table from Griff, Shari felt more secure and since his talk was all of horses, she began, insensibly, to relax.

'Tell me some more about your uncle's Haflingers,' she suggested, when the conversation seemed to be in danger of flagging and her drink too hot to finish at a gulp.

'They've been known in this country since 1959. The Duke and Duchess of Devonshire bought some for work on their estate, hauling timber, where a tractor couldn't go. In the Tyrol, Haflingers are used for ploughing, cultivating, haymaking and harvesting. The Devonshires formed a society of owners, "The Haflinger Society of Great Britain". My uncle Geoffrey's a member. Their main aim is to preserve the pedigree, hence Geoff's disgust when his mare ran amok.'

'Are they shown at all?' Shari asked, completely absorbed.

'There's an annual breed show, and Haflingers are

eligible to take part in driving classes, or other classes not specifically confined to British mountain and moorland breeds.'

'I suppose, crossed with a fell-pony, you could get a marvellously strong, steady strain, ideal for pony trekking?'

'Mmm, and for disabled riders too.' He put down his empty mug with an air of finality. 'And now *we* are going to bed.'

Again she knew a tremor at his method of expressing himself, even though she knew that was all it was, but she did allow herself a fleeting moment, to wonder what it would be like, to be going to bed with Griff.

'What's up with you?' he asked, with one of his occasional, uncomfortable flashes of perception. 'You're as pink as a peony. *You didn't think* . . .?' he began and, as automatically she began to shake her head. 'Oh yes you did, otherwise you wouldn't know what I mean.'

She tried to sidestep him, but he was too adroit for her.

'Relax, Shari.' His tone was amused, indulgent, as he took her in his arms. 'I've no designs on you, except, perhaps,' he said softly, thoughtfully, 'to kiss you good night.'

'Don't you think you've done enough of that? You shouldn't, you mustn't, because . . .'

'But I'm going to!' he interrupted her distraught protests and then there was no further opportunity to voice them, his lips stilling hers, their touch as light as the brush of a butterfly's wings, in no way threatening, but still as discomposing. Even that brief touch was enough to quicken her heartbeat. She wanted him to kiss her properly now, wanted it with a burning need; but already he was putting her from him, shooing her towards the stairs with what seemed like a patronising slap upon her behind.

'Bed!' he commanded. 'And don't oversleep in the

morning. We have four horses to muck out now, you and I.'

That last delightful conjunction of words sent her to bed unreasonably happy, an unreason which did not last, because it was not long before realisation dawned. Griff's bringing his horses here could only mean one thing, that Estelle's purchase of Threlkeld was now a certainty, could take place at any moment, and then there would be a wedding.

With a sudden, angry sound that was suspiciously like a sob, she began to pull off the borrowed clothes and flung herself into bed, praying for immediate oblivion, release from such tortured imaginings.

'Are you trying to break a record, or just that fork?'

Shari paused in her frenetic attack on the soiled straw in Rainbow's loose-box. Jimmy was leaning against the doorpost, his nice-looking face alight with amusement. She threw down her fork and went to join him, face flushed from exertions, but also with the indignation to which she now gave voice.

'I'm beginning to think that the sooner the sale of this place goes through the better it will be!'

Jimmy's amiable features contorted in surprise.

'Are you sure you know what you're saying?'

'Yes! We have to sell, O.K.? And if Estelle's definitely buying, then I want out.'

'But I thought you'd adopted a policy of avoidance, that all your dealings were with Griff?'

'That's true,' she conceded, 'but since Estelle seems to have got him "right here",' she gestured expressively with her thumb, 'it seems to me that I'm still taking *her* orders, even if only second-hand.'

'So what brought on this particular fit of rebellion?'

Shari pointed to the area she was cleaning out and to the three other occupied boxes, to which she had already attended.

'The idea was that Griff and I should share the mucking out. But is he here?' It was a rhetorical question and Jimmy recognised it as such, wisely leaving it unanswered. 'No, he isn't! Because Madame Estelle decided she wanted him to drive her somewhere so Muggins here was left to do the lot.'

'You know I'd have given you a hand,' Jimmy said. 'Why didn't you ask?'

'Because I know they're keeping you busy too, and besides, it's not the work I object to. I love horses. It's just the principle of the thing ... and *her* high-handed ways.'

'I suppose she *has* got first call on his time,' Jimmy pointed out.

Shari digested this bitter pill.

'Yes,' she admitted unwillingly.

Jimmy wandered along the row of boxes, giving a word and a caress to each occupant.

'He's got some fine animals here. D'you know what he's got in mind for them?'

Shari gave him the gist of what Griff had told her.

'So it looks as if the takeover can't be far distant then,' he commented. 'He'd hardly take the trouble otherwise to ship his horses all the way up here.'

Shari had already worked this out for herself, but her heart sank anew at hearing it reiterated.

'I'll have to find myself digs in the village,' Jimmy went on. 'There won't be room for me in the cottage my Gran and yours will be sharing. How about you?'

'I shall be leaving Beckdale.' She returned to her fierce attack upon the soiled straw.

'Oh no!' He was dismayed. 'But why? I thought you liked the idea of working with Griff's horses?'

'I did, but I've changed my mind.'

'And I think I know why. It's not the job you've changed your mind about, is it? It's because you can't face the idea of seeing Griff married to Estelle.'

'I couldn't care less who he marries,' she began; then her voice trailed away and she turned her back on Jimmy knowing that her compressed lips and over-bright eyes would betray her.

'Who are you kidding? I've seen this coming, right from the start. You're in love with him, yes?'

'Even if I was,' she said carefully, 'and I'm not saying that I am, it wouldn't do me any good. He belongs to Estelle.'

'Does he? It seems to me that Griff Masterson is very much his own man. It may look as if he's under her thumb but nine-tenths of him is below the surface! Shari, don't allow yourself to get hurt like this, why not fight back? Go all out for what you want.'

'Dear Jimmy, you're a good pal, but you needn't worry about me. I'm a survivor.' Wearily, 'I've got to be, haven't I?' She stood on tiptoe and brushed his cheek with her lips.

'I'm sorry, I didn't realise we'd be interrupting anything!' A voice had Shari springing away as if she were guilty of some misdemeanour. Estelle and Griff had come upon them unnoticed. Estelle looked merely amused, but Griff's face was set in an unreadable expression.

Embarrassed by the obvious misunderstanding, Jimmy turned and hurried away muttering something about having work to do; but Shari stood her ground. She was glad, she told herself fiercely, that Griff had seen. It would do much to correct the impression he undoubtedly had that she was ready and willing for *his* kisses.

'I see you've finished mucking out,' Griff observed. 'You work fast. I had hoped to be back in time.'

'Horses' needs can't wait indefinitely upon pleasure trips,' she said casually, swinging back towards Rainbow's stall.

'Pleasure trip!' It was Estelle's high drawl that

answered her. 'Yes, I suppose it was for us, though I don't suppose our errand will give *you* much pleasure.'

Shari froze, her back still turned upon the couple.

'We've submitted our planning application to make alterations and additions to the property,' Estelle continued. 'Once we receive the go-ahead we can go about buying Threlkeld.'

Shari was able to move again; to her it seemed as if she had been visibly riveted to the spot, but in reality her pause had been infinitesimal. The news wasn't good, but it could have been far, far worse.

'Oh!' she said, forcing deliberate lack of interest into her voice. 'And is that likely to take long?'

'The planning committee doesn't meet for another six weeks,' Griff said, 'so it will be some time before we have any definite news.'

'And do you intend to go on staying here for that six weeks?' Her grandmother would be grateful for the extra income during this period of decision, but six weeks! Another six weeks of their disruptive presence about the place, Estelle's exacerbating to her nerves, but Griff's . . .! Goodness only knew what six more weeks of *his* company would do to her.

'Yes. Your grandmother has kindly agreed to let us continue as paying guests. Estelle means to stay on full-time,' she heard him say. 'But I mustn't neglect my business interests that long. There's a great deal to be wound up before I finally move north.' He sounded very certain that the move would be made. He couldn't have much doubt that planning permission would be granted.

He was going away again. She had feared the continuation of his presence, now she dreaded his absence. But it would give her time to look around for a job. By the time he returned she would be able to face him coolly, would have arranged her departure.

'So I shall be up just at weekends.' With a few words he destroyed her plans, shook her resolve; for her traitorous heart jolted upwards at the reprieve. 'I'll make arrangements for one of the men to help with the heavy work in the yard, but I'd like you to exercise the horses for me, except Rusty.'

'Why not Rusty?' she exclaimed. She was much drawn to the attractively coloured, half-bred Haflinger.

'Because,' Griff said drily, 'he's a strong beast to handle. He's a stallion.'

Uncomprehendingly, she stared at him and his tongue gave a click of exasperation. 'I didn't think I'd have to spell it out for a country-bred girl. If a stallion gets scent of any mares nearby, and I hope to have those ponies in the two-acre field in a day or so, it takes a firm hand to restrain him. Jimmy will exercise Rusty.'

As he spoke, the colour had risen in her cheeks and she was further mortified by the sound of Estelle's chuckle.

'Even I know that and I've no time for the wretched animals.'

Stung to retort, Shari pulled no punches.

'What a good thing! Since no self-respecting animal would want anything to do with you either!'

'Shari!' Griff's voice was curt and she turned on him too.

'And you needn't think I'm going to be bullied into apologising this time. Your girlfriend would like to see me out of Threlkeld anyway, so I'm giving her a helping hand. I'm looking for another job and as soon as I see my grandmother settled, I'm off.'

'Where to?' he demanded sharply.

'I don't think that really concerns you.' Estelle must have gained great satisfaction from her words, Shari thought bitterly, as she watched the other woman walk away. Despite Griff's abrupt question he probably didn't care whether she left or not. To him she was only a useful employee, a stable-lad.

Only once had he betrayed any actual physical

response during their kisses and that had been *her* fault, practically throwing herself at him, making him think she was . . . She *had* to believe that she meant nothing more to him than a few minutes' idle dalliance. It was the only way she could begin to cure herself of the desperate craving that had possessed her these last few weeks.

'I see!' Griff was saying now, his tone carefully controlled. 'I had thought that we'd resolved all that nonsense, that you, and Jimmy too, were going to stay on here as much for the sake of your grandmothers as anything else. I can't understand why *you* should suddenly change your mind.'

No, she thought wearily; he wouldn't understand, because he had no idea of what he'd done to her.

'Well, I *have* changed my mind. And now, you'll have to excuse me. I've finished feeding and mucking out, but these horses still have to be exercised.'

'That won't take long, now that I'm here. We'll take Jet and Conker out together, then Rusty and Rainbow.'

She didn't want him to come with her, but could think of no reasonable objection. In silence, she saddled up the sprightly black mare; and a pang ran through her, as she realised that if she carried out her avowed intent, she wouldn't be here to ride the mare in the jumping events at August's show.

Griff led Conker out of his box. The chestnut gelding had a good-looking head, strong shoulders, back and hocks, ideal for the necessary impulsion to carry him clearly round a jumping arena.

'Need a leg up?' Griff asked.

'No!' She didn't want him to touch her. She amended it to 'No thank you. I can manage.'

It was a beautiful morning for a ride amidst the sylvan beauty of the lakes and dales. In single file at first, they followed the line of a beck, the clear water sliding over green weed, but as the trail widened, Griff slowed his mount to let Shari come alongside.

'Well, what do you think of her?' He jerked his head towards the mare.

'She's superb; she has a lovely action. I wish she were mine.'

'If you were to stay, she could be,' he said tersely, adding, 'in all but name. I was hoping you'd ride her in local events for me.'

Their route took them along a well-worn track of woodland path, the horses' footfalls deadened by the accumulated leaf-mould of years, and still Shari had no answer for him.

'I wish,' he said irritably after a while, 'that you'd give me some good reason for wanting to leave. *Is* it just the problem of Estelle owning Threlkeld? Because . . .'

'No!' She interrupted him before he could delve more deeply. 'I don't like the idea, naturally, but it's more than that.' Desperately, she invented. 'I've decided, a bit belatedly perhaps, to take some advice my grandmother gave me years ago. She said it would be criminal to spend the whole of my life in one place. I've suddenly realised she's right. There's a great big world out there,' she gestured beyond the charmed circle of the mountains, 'that I've hardly seen.'

'And you mean to see it?'

'Yes.' If things had been different, Shari knew she would count the rest of the fascinating world well lost.

'Is there nothing I can say, or do, to persuade you to change your mind?'

Only tell me you've changed *your* mind, that you're not going to marry Estelle, was her unspoken answer.

Her continuing silence seemed to aggravate him. Stealing a sideways glance at his profile, she saw it taut, tight-lipped, a cold, angry mask. Yet why should he be so incensed by her alleged determination? Even with her love of horses, her local knowledge, she wasn't irreplaceable; her leaving wouldn't interfere with his plans.

'We'd better turn back now, if we're to exercise the other pair.' With an abrupt movement he reined back and, her mare still moving forward, Shari felt leg and arm brush his. Before she could ease Jet away, a strong hand clamped on the bridle and, startled, she turned to look up at Griff, surprising an odd expression on his face, one of strain about the well-shaped mouth and the sapphire-blue eyes.

'I have to go back to London tomorrow, Shari. I'll be gone for a month.'

'I thought you were coming back every weekend,' she cried involuntarily, not realising the dismay revealed in her widely spaced eyes, the droop of her mouth.

'I think perhaps it would be as well if I didn't,' he said gruffly. 'The more concentrated effort I put into winding up my affairs there, the sooner I'll be back here, on the spot permanently. Whether or not we buy Threlkeld, I intend to live somewhere in this area, carry out my breeding ideas. Perhaps when I come back . . .' He stopped and then, with what she was certain was a change of subject, continued, 'I intend to be back in July anyway, for the sheep-shearing. I shall,' he added stiffly, 'still pay the agreed rental for my room.'

'I don't think my grandmother would expect, or allow, you to do that,' was her cold reply.

'Nevertheless!'

They rode back in silence. Only as they turned into the stableyard did Griff say, brusquely,

'During the next month, while I'm away, give a little more thought to your plans. Don't do anything hasty. You may change your mind.'

'I doubt it.' She pulled off her hard hat, freeing her long black hair to fall about her shoulders, a misty curtain, half obscuring her profile from him. Then, sliding from the saddle, she found him before her, his arms waiting to receive her. Too late to halt her descent, she found herself very close to him, her retreat cut off by Jet's silky black flanks. 'Please, let me pass,' she began.

'Why? What's your rush? What are you afraid of?'

'I'm not. It's just that we have to rub down the horses, and there are two more waiting to be exercised, and I . . .'

'You *are* afraid!' he accused. 'For some reason you're afraid of *me*! What possible reason have I given you to fear me?'

Faint colour stained her high, clearly modelled cheekbones and she evaded his eyes.

'Please, Griff, don't!' she whispered.

Amazingly, unexpectedly, he stood aside and at once she felt a chill of the spirits. She hadn't thought he would give in so easily, and contrarily she realised that she had *wanted* him to restrain her. As she passed him, her legs tremulous, he reached out and grasped a handful of her dark hair, temporarily halting her progress.

'You remind me of Jet,' he said astonishingly. 'When I first bought her, *she* was skittish, nervous, too wild to handle,' he added softly. Then, as she stared speechlessly at him, torn by the aching longing of her senses, awakened as she had known they would be by his slightest touch, he added, 'But I'm a patient man, I tamed *her*. It took me a long time, but there was pleasure in the act of subjugation, in bending a wild, untamed creature to my will.'

Aware of breathlessness, still mesmerised by the hold on her of hand and eye, Shari could not move, until he released her, with the quietly spoken words,

'Are you too wild to hold? Somehow, in spite of your "don't touch me" manner, I don't think so, and I'll tame you yet!'

CHAPTER SIX

THE fellside echoed to the blaring protest of the harassed Herdwick. The flock of jostling animals would have been quite happy to move at a sheep's pace on this sleepy summer afternoon; but the dogs had other ideas.

Today the whole of Threlkeld's resources were concentrated upon the July shearing. For the men the hard, hot, back-breaking work of denuding the struggling animals; for the women, the constant supply of refreshments. These latter, Shari noticed, comprised herself and Lily Crosthwaite, plus the wives of the farm workers.

Griff's absence had seemed endless to Shari, more so than on the previous occasion. Then, she had not yet realised the depths of her feelings for him. Now that she knew the sensations he aroused in her were those of love, of an intolerable, aching desire, the days had been harder to bear, even though she had deliberately filled their hours to capacity. Though her heart was not really in the task, she had written off for various jobs. She had even been granted one or two interviews, but without success.

Never had horses been as well looked after as the four in her care and her only regret was that Griff had not had time before his departure to arrange for the purchase of the fell ponies he wanted for breeding-stock and for trekking. She would have liked to have the care of them, just for a little while.

He had returned yesterday in time, as he had promised, for the first day of the shearing, and to her amazement she found that he intended to take a part in the proceedings.

'I've done so many times before, on my father's farm,' he told her, when she expressed surprise. 'I believe a farmer *should* be able to tackle any job he expects his men to do.'

She looked at him now, his upper torso exposed to the sunlight that streamed down across the hills and scorched the farmyard with its rays. He was bronzed already, she noticed, unable to drag her eyes from the sight of his smooth skin, the hair on which was bleached as pale as that on his head. His chest and arms were muscular, but pleasantly so; she hated the excessively bulging muscles of body-builders. She knew she should be in the kitchen, supervising the great tea-urn, which only came out on such occasions as shearing and harvesting. But curiosity compelled her to remain. She had to see what kind of hand Griff made at his self-imposed task.

She had not been alone with him since his return; and she could not decide if this was a matter for relief or regret. He had not referred to her plan to leave Threlkeld, nor had he asked her if she'd done as he'd requested, reconsidered her intention.

Some of the men were sitting on benches now, sacks draped across their knees and between their legs. Each held a sheep, the beasts looking ridiculously ineffectual and undignified in their spreadeagled, upside-down position, their heads held in a grip like a wrestling hold from which they could not escape. Though she had witnessed this operation year after year since childhood, the sight never ceased to fascinate Shari, the almost rhythmical, efficient stripping of fleeces, that seemed to come away with the ease of peeling an orange, until the sheep, released once more, dipped and re-marked with an identifying dye, trotted away, almost pathetic in their bewildered, dripping nakedness. But this year, there was an added, compelling interest and she felt a curious sense of pride that Griff could keep pace with the other men, the pile of fleeces around him growing as rapidly as theirs.

The sight of the men's perspiring faces recalled Shari to a sense of duty and soon she re-emerged from the kitchen, carrying a large teapot, Lily following behind with a tray set with mugs. During this welcome break for the men, Shari wished she could think of an excuse to linger by Griff, to make conversation, but he took his tea from her, dismissing her with a brief word of thanks.

At the end of the day's shearing, as was the usual custom, a supper was provided in the farm kitchen for the shearers and for their wives, who had been too busy to prepare individual meals for their men. Shari and her grandmother always attended these suppers, which, despite the men's fatigue, always seemed to develop into merry occasions. There were always humorous incidents of the day to be related, individual tallies of fleeces to be bragged about.

Shari found Griff seated beside her. Like the other men, his face was drawn with fatigue, but it was a contented tiredness, she knew, as though with the sense of a day's work well done, and without being told, she knew also that he had relished every moment of it.

'You're going to enjoy being a farmer, aren't you?' she asked him under cover of the noisy, general conversation.

'If things work out as I plan, yes!'

Whilst Griff had been away, she had heard rumours of a protest going around Beckdale, of a petition being drawn up, opposing the use to which Griff and Estelle proposed to put Threlkeld Hall. She knew that several of the farmhands had threatened to find other employment if the scheme went through, even though their cottage homes were tied to their job. It would be a terrible shame if Threlkeld lost men whose fathers and grandfathers before them had worked for the Freemans.

She wondered if Estelle had got wind of the petition and if she had told Griff. She asked him.

'Yes. I've heard about it.' He didn't seem unduly perturbed, she thought. But he was probably confident that permission would be granted. Why should he care? she thought, trying to lash herself into a state of aggrieved resentment, what happened to families who had been in Beckdale before *he* was born?

But she couldn't help probing the wound.

'What will you do about it?'

'Do?' He leant back in his chair, stretching, flexing tired muscles, his shoulder brushing hers, making hot awareness run through her. 'I'll do what I would have done in any case, wait and see what happens.' He grinned at her irritated exclamation and changed the subject. 'How have the horses been shaping up? Are you getting on all right with Jet?'

'Oh yes!' At once she was all animation, violet eyes sparkling, animosity temporarily forgotten in enthusiasm. 'But she's very impetuous, and so lively. She has no sense of decorum over the jumps.'

Griff laughed.

'She used to be my sister's horse, and you've just described Naomi to a T. Naomi and Jet's progress around an arena was very much a hit-and-miss affair. I hope you'll be able to teach her better manners.'

'Why doesn't your sister ride her any more?' Shari couldn't imagine anyone wanting to part with the delicate-limbed yet spunky mare.

'She lives abroad now she's married; my mother doesn't ride, so bringing Jet here was the ideal alternative to selling her, something I was reluctant to do. Did you do as I asked about Rusty? You let *Jimmy* exercise him?' His blue gaze was penetrating and she was glad she could answer truthfully, albeit regretfully.

'Yes, but I *wish* you'd let me ride him. He hasn't caused Jimmy a spot of trouble, even when we've had him out with Jet. He seems to know that he must keep his mind on work when he's being ridden.'

'Nevertheless, I don't want *you* riding him,' Griff reiterated, 'and,' with a grin, 'his *other* duties will begin soon. In the next two or three days, I've got half a dozen ponies, all mares, coming over from that chap at Kendal.'

'What about the ones Charlie promised you?'

'Ah, now.' He looked at her, a provocative half-smile on his lips, a smile that had the power to make her heart perform strange gymnastics. 'That's where *you* come in. After my last encounter with Charlie Garner, I have the distinct impression that I shall need your personal recommendation before he'll part with a single animal.'

Shari coloured slightly, remembering the threats Griff had made that day and the way in which he had carried them out. She had a chance here, if she cared to take it, to avenge those indignities, but she knew she wouldn't.

'And if I *won't* give you a reference?' she asked, unaware of the betraying, lovely wicked twinkle in her eyes.

'Oh, I think I'll be able to persuade you!' he said softly, suggestively, his own eyes silver-sparked with amusement at her renewed confusion.

Shari decided there and then that no persuasion of the nature he hinted at should be necessary.

'I'll have a word with Charlie. I'll tell him you're not really the ogre you appear to be.'

'It must be the hottest day of the year,' Shari gasped, as she and Griff rode out towards the Garner farm. He nodded agreement, then, 'Have you thought any more about your future plans?'

'I've thought about it a lot,' she admitted. 'I still think it would be better if I went.' She waited for some outburst from him, some attempt at persuasion; and she was disconcerted when he made no immediate comment. She risked a surreptitious look at him, only to find him scrutinising her face intently, a curious expression in those unusually vivid eyes.

'If only I knew for sure,' he began; but irritatingly, he did not complete his sentence and as Shari waited for him to do so, he urged Conker onwards, the chestnut gelding responding willingly in spite of the heat, whilst Shari, disappointed, her curiosity unsatisfied, followed more slowly in his wake.

Charlie Garner was inclined to be stiff and hostile at first, blue eyes wary, white moustache bristling; but after narrowly watching Shari's deliberately easy, friendly manner with Griff, he unbent sufficiently to suggest that they might walk up the fell at the back of the farmhouse and take a look at his mares.

On the hillside, a calm, warm peace prevailed, broken only by the soft sounds of mild breezes combing through dry grass, until they came upon the ponies, which, startled by the arrival of strangers, snorted and scampered away, their hooves thumping irregularly on the hard ground. From a safe distance, they regarded the human interlopers, bright little eyes flashing, tails flickering noiselessly from side to side. They were adorable creatures, Shari thought, rough and shaggy, sturdy, their abounding health evident in their sharp, alert movements.

'Oh yes, they're tame,' Charlie said in response to a question from Griff. 'But you two are strangers to them. Once you've fed them a couple of times, they'll come to you readily enough. Wait here and watch.' Slowly, he moved towards the little group. The animals watched him, ears twitching, nostrils quivering inquisitively. He felt in his pocket, then held out a hand in front of him. As Charlie moved closer still, Shari found she was holding her breath, releasing it on a sigh of relief as one pony, bolder than the rest, investigated the outstretched hand. Then the ponies were clustered about the elderly farmer, recognising his familiar odour, nosing at his pockets for the sugar he always carried.

Once the ponies had been reassured, they allowed Griff and Shari to approach. Gently but firmly, she ran her hands over one of the mares, good, firm flesh. But then Charlie always had looked after his livestock.

By now there seemed to be no doubt that Charlie would sell six of his mares to Griff and when they left, arrangements had been made for their delivery to Threlkeld the following week.

'Now,' Griff said, as they rode away, 'is there anywhere we can cool off in this infernal heat, anywhere we can swim?'

'There *is* somewhere,' she began, 'but we've no costumes.'

Griff surveyed her jeans and short-sleeved blouse with an assessing, knowledgeable eye.

'I daresay what you have on under there is as decent as any bikini?'

'Yes, but . . .'

'And I assure you I'm similarly respectable . . . so where is this place?'

She might as well show him. *He* could go in if he liked. *She* didn't have to, much as she yearned to feel the cooling silk of mountain water on her flesh. *She* would mind the horses . . . *and* turn her back, she vowed.

'It's in what we call the Hidden Valley,' she told him. 'Nobody much goes there, only local people, and they're usually too busy at this time of day.'

'So we're likely to have it to ourselves?' There was a strange note in his voice which she could not interpret, which gave her a sense of unease, but she nodded.

'Then what are we waiting for? Lead on,' he commanded.

Pegdale was enclosed by a long ridge of fells that discouraged casual visitors. There was a narrow entry, but no signpost indicated its whereabouts and Shari always thought that it must look exactly as it had done fifty or a hundred years ago, a long, green valley bisected by a small, clear tarn. On this still day there were no other sights or sounds but the occasional bleat of a sheep, the call of a curlew. Despite the recent dry weather, a thin trickle of moisture still tumbled down a beck, to join the inviting waters of the tarn, which Shari knew from experience would be exhilaratingly cold and fresh.

'Better tie the horses up,' Griff said, pointing to a handily placed rowan tree. 'I'd hate to have to walk home in this heat.'

She made a lengthy, assiduous task of it, hearing faint sounds from behind her that told her he was stripping off jeans and shirt. She wouldn't turn round yet, not until he was in the water.

She heard the splash as the water welcomed his body, could imagine the delight his heated flesh must feel at its laving coolness. The thought made her own body feel hotter by comparison. To add to her torture, she could hear the faint tinkle of sliding pebbles, caused by the thin gurgle of the beck.

'Come on, Shari!' She heard Griff's impatient urging. 'It's marvellous.'

She turned, reluctantly, relieved to see that only his blond head showed above the surface of the water.

'I'm not coming in,' she called, 'I'll just sit here and wait.' She threw herself down on the turf, trying to look comfortably relaxed.

He came to the edge, the water level receding as he advanced until it was just below waist level.

'You'll get heat stroke sitting there, and I don't intend to come out just yet.'

'In that case, I'll take Jet and ride on,' she suggested.

'You can follow when you're ready.' She began to rise, but as she did so, he plunged out of the pool, the water draining from him, flattening soft, light hairs to his muscular thighs and calves, moulding his brief shorts to his body. Hastily, she averted her eyes and in a wild rush completed the scramble to her feet.

A strong, wet hand closed about her forearm, yanking her off balance.

'You contrary little . . . get your clothes off and get in that water. That's an order!'

'You're not my boss yet, you can't . . .'

'Are you going to do as I say?'

'No, I . . .'

'Right!' With complete indifference to her protests, he bent and scooped her up into his arms. The scent of him came to her . . . male warmth mingled with the freshness of the water droplets, a lingering trace of body cologne. His grasp upon her was firm, hard, and she felt herself go tense in an effort not to betray the unbearable sexual excitement mounting rapidly within her. As he strode with her towards the water's edge, she guessed his intent and began her struggles again. But she was no match for his determination. With an easy movement of his arms he released and threw her towards the centre of the tarn, the shock as her body cleaved the clear, cold water making her gasp and shout her indignation aloud, filling her mouth and nose.

Down she sank, disturbing a shoal of minnows, down among the slow, sleepy undulation of weeds. The idea came to her in a flash of mischievous inspiration. He could have drowned her. He wasn't to know that she *could* swim. She'd give him the fright of his life.

Her head broke the water and she emptied her mouth, kept her eyes shut and breathed in deeply, before allowing herself to sink once more, her hands thrown up in the classical pose of one drowning. As she went through this artistic performance for the third time, she felt the water near her disturbed by his dive, felt him drawing her up to the surface, swimming for the edge, her body held in a lifesaving position.

With an effort, she managed to subdue the laughter that bubbled up within her, threatening to betray her. It had worked; and she hoped he was thoroughly scared by the outcome of his rash action. It wasn't difficult to remain totally limp as he hauled her out on to the grassy edge.

But after a while, she was beginning to find that the joke was on her. Flat on her stomach, head turned to one side, she was violently conscious of Griff astride her, the strong grip of his inner thighs, the rhythmic pressure of his hands upon her back. She allowed water to trickle from her mouth and essayed a tiny sigh of sound. It would be better, for the sake of her pounding pulses, to make a swift recovery. He moved, turning her over, his head at her breast now, listening, and she knew a fervid longing to clasp that damp head with both hands and keep it there. Evidently satisfied by the strength of the beat he heard—to her it seemed unnaturally accelerated—he looked up and encountered her eyes watching him.

'Shari!' He took her gently by the shoulders. 'My God! I'm sorry! But why didn't you tell me you couldn't swim? Are you all right?'

She could only nod. He was so close, the brief garment that he wore leaving so little to the imagination that a convulsive spasm worked her throat.

'I'd better get you home! Here, take off those wet clothes. You can wear mine, we'll have to roll the sleeves and trouser legs up, but ...' He made a movement to unbutton her blouse, but she was too quick for him.

'No,' she gasped, 'there's no need. I'll be perfectly all right like this. The sun will soon dry me.'

'You ought to have dry clothes on,' he argued,

'you're in shock. Allow me to know what's best for you.' Holding both her hands in one of his, he made a fresh onslaught upon the buttons and immediately Shari capitulated.

'All right, all right, but *I'll* do it.'

He insisted on helping to her feet, his sapphire eyes still watching her with concern.

'Honestly, Shari, I thought you could swim. Please believe me, I'd never . . .'

'Would you please look the other way,' she demanded stiffly. Conscience was beginning to prick her. She hadn't actually *told* a lie, but she'd acted one, and it bothered her.

'Come on!' he said impatiently. 'You're being unnecessarily prudish. If this were a beach, you wouldn't think twice.'

Wherever she was, she'd think *more* than twice about exposing herself to *his* gaze, Shari thought, and nylon underwear was hardly as protective as a bikini manufactured specially for the purpose.

Her fingers trembled as she fumbled with buttons and zip and she kept her eyes averted from Griff, even though she knew instinctively that *his* eyes were fixed on her. So acutely tuned were her senses that she even heard the slight intake of his breath as she shed the last of her wet outer garments.

Her downcast eyes caught the movement of his strong bare feet on the turf and at once she looked up, alarm springing afresh, as she caught the unguarded expression on his face. Shari was not vain, but she knew her figure, though petite, was well proportioned, and interpreting his advance correctly, she knew that the sight of her had aroused him. Just the thought of what he might do when he drew nearer made her legs feel as weak as though she really were recovering from shock; and a sudden tightness in the cups of her bra made her shamingly aware of the swelling of her breasts, the straining tips visible through the thinness of the material.

One appalled glance and she fled towards the nearest retreat, the cold, douching, common sense of the tarn, which might quell the fiery longings that invaded her. Without understanding, she heard Griff's frantic shout, but as she took a neat dive into the water, propelling herself towards the centre of the tarn, with strong overarm strokes, she realised that she had given herself away. Now he knew she could swim, and he wasn't going to like having been made a fool of. Morever she didn't stand an icicle in hell's chance of avoiding retribution.

The thrash of her own limbs upon the water drowned the sounds of pursuit, but with the certainty of one in a nightmare she knew he was on her trail. Her limbs, suddenly tremulous, seemed incapable of forwarding her progress.

She had no alternative but to turn and face the music.

Treading water, she brushed the wet dark hair aside from her face and scanned the surface. She looked towards the edge, the horses still grazed peacefully. He wasn't there. She was certain he had entered the water in pursuit of her. He should have come up on her by now. Sudden fear smote her. Suppose he suffered with cramp? All the time she had been supposedly fleeing from him, he might have been drowning.

She took a deep breath, preparatory to diving, then felt a tremendous pull upon her dangling legs. She was thankful for the air she had inhaled, as she found herself below the surface, being hauled inexorably deeper, until her face was on a level with Griff's.

Beneath the water his wide-open eyes were as unfathomable as the tarn itself, his compressed mouth grim. Then he pulled her against him and she knew immediately that immersion had not quenched the fire in either of them. The erotic, throbbing pressure of his aroused body against hers was an instant, sweet torment, the thrust of his leg between hers a deliberate, punishing provocation.

Together they broke surface, his lips mated with hers and with one arm holding her captive, the powerful thrust of the other and of his churning legs took them to the side, their bodies still as if fused together.

They lay just at the water's edge, its coolness still lapping around their ankles as his mouth probed hers, lingeringly, marvellously intense in its exploration. She knew she was trembling, felt him tremble too. One hand cupped a breast that came to life at his touch, the wetness of the thin material making its protection as ineffectual as if it did not exist. She had never been touched like this before. *He* had never touched her this way.

It seemed that he drew her closer yet, the wet warmth, the tender suppleness of naked bodies melded together. The feel of his hard, masculine presence against her, the skilful pressures he was exerting, made her senses ache with longing.

She had never caressed a man before. Now she ran exploratory hands over the smoothness of his back, traced the route of his spine from its base to the nape of his neck, wound her fingers in among the damp strands of hair.

He released the back fastening of her bra and she felt the sodden material peel away, felt the warm, sultry air delicious on her skin, replaced by the warmer touch of his hand, his lips. She shuddered with unendurable pleasure. She felt so much, and yet it was not enough. She wanted more and more of him, his kisses, his caresses, she wanted *him*, totally.

She responded more fiercely to his ardour, every sense willing to surrender to his demands. This burning ache could only be appeased by the one who had aroused it.

Then, slowly, lingeringly, incredibly, he began to

draw away from her, as if he could hardly bring himself to do so, but his intent was still obvious and she groaned an entreaty that clearly betrayed her sense of deprivation. Unwittingly, innocently wanton, she tried to press herself to him once more, unassuaged starvation gnawing at her inner being. But he was firm with her now, holding her away from him, then rolling over in one swift movement that took him also to his feet and back into the tarn, where he swam away from her, with a strength that seemed tinged with desperation.

Shari sat up, bunching her knees, her arms curled around them, stomach muscles painfully contracted as she fought an inner agony. Common sense began to reassert itself and with it came shame, as she realised just how badly she had behaved, how she had given in to the pull of physical need. She had no right to demand its fulfilment from this man, nor he the right to give it to her. And *he* had been the one to recall that fact. How he must despise her for her easy capitulation; and yet she knew that if, at this moment, he again attempted to take her in his arms, she would go, weakly, unresistingly. Love and guilt mingled, wrapped her in a confusion of emotions, so torn and confused that she could not speak, when he left the water once more and came towards her, his expression wary.

Was he afraid that she would throw herself at him? Or did he anticipate reproach?

Spurred on by her shame and the pride now ascendant, she turned and picked up her clothes. She dressed quickly, not looking in his direction, but knowing that he was doing the same.

Despite the warmth her fingers felt strangely numb as she tried to free the tether that held Jet to the tree; and she could not hurry the process though she longed to be astride her mount, to ride away from this now humiliating scene. But Griff was beside her, his own horse released first, and then he was helping her. She kept her face averted. Reaction was setting in and she felt perilously close to tears, tears of frustration. However he had behaved in the last few moments she loved him as much as ever, and this afternoon had shown her clearly just how much.

A strong hand cupped her chin, forcing it round, lifting it.

'I'm sorry, Shari, don't cry, love. I nearly ... we nearly ... but I never intended ...' Then, seeing the threatening tears spill over, he gave a deep groan and pulled her roughly against his chest. 'Did I hurt you? Frighten you? Shock you? Shari, believe me, I wouldn't have. It wouldn't have gone any further.'

But *I* wanted it to, she cried inwardly, knowing that this made her more despicable than he. She leant against him, totally spent, incapable of any further feeling, so traumatic had these last few seconds since his rejection been.

His voice went on above her head, its tone as gentle as the hand that caressed the still damp black tresses.

'I *know* though you're a woman in years you're still young and innocent, unawakened, just a half-wild creature.'

I'm *not* unawakened, not now, she thought, not any more; but he went on,

'I should never have behaved as I did ... but,' he held her a little away, looking down into her face, a wry smile creasing his rugged features, 'but you did rather ask for it you know, pretending you were drowning. You deserved some kind of punishment.'

If only he were to be the one to administer correction, she thought half hysterically, she could well take to a whole life of crime. Violet eyes still swimming in tears, she looked up at him. She had no idea of the pleading invitation of her quivering mouth, the tremulous fluttering of her body beneath his hands. He shook his head, half ruefully, his words mystifying her.

'No, little Shari, not yet. You're not ready, and neither am I. My plans didn't include ...' He stopped and with another negative movement of his head he released her.

Slowly the horses followed the homeward trail. She would never feel the same again about swimming in a mountain tarn, Shari thought listlessly. On every other occasion she had felt like a giant refreshed, but now she felt engulfed in a fatiguing lethargy that, did she but know it, was more of the spirit than of the body. She doubted, in fact, if she would ever visit that particular valley again; it was as if its encircling ridges would always encapsulate for her the sensations and emotions she had experienced there.

Griff kept his mount alongside hers and she was aware that from time to time, he glanced at her. Did he guess what she was going through? Awful, final humiliation!

'Not speaking to me?' he enquired after a while; his tone was an attempt at teasing, but she sensed the anxiety beneath. What did *he* care whether or not she ever spoke to him again.

'What is there to say?'

'That you've forgiven me?' he suggested. 'That we're still friends?'

She was silent, her eyes fixed determinedly ahead of her on the serene, peaceful valley of Beckdale. Near at hand, butterflies were busy among the clover and in one of the fields near the farm, sunburned men were turning hay. In another, yellow-green in the sunlight, piled bales cast long, sharp shadows. Until now this countryside had represented all that was perfect, a sleepy contentment, until Estelle and Griff, the off-comers, had arrived to disturb its tranquillity. She spoke out of these thoughts, emphatically.

'I can *never* forgive you, never!'

She risked a sideways glance, to see how he had taken her reply. His profile was cold, remote—a little white about the mouth? He was probably tired. It had been an exhausting day physically.

They clattered into the yard and as if their arrival had been the signal for which everyone was waiting; several doors flew open simultaneously, that of Jimmy's office, the kitchen door, revealing Lily Crosthwaite—from her expression agog with news—and the side door to the house, from which Estelle emerged; and it was all too obvious that *she* was in a towering rage.

Seeing Estelle, Lily withdrew, but Jimmy advanced across the yard to stand at Jet's head.

Estelle too made straight for the riders, turning a high heel on the cobbles in her haste, a painful incident which would certainly not improve her mood. Shari began to urge Jet forward. She felt in no mood for listening to the other woman's problems; she had enough of her own. But the high, imperious voice halted her progress.

'Shari Freeman! Stay right where you are! You obnoxious, underhand, scheming little bitch!'

Shari felt the blood drain from her face. Had Estelle somehow found out about the events of the afternoon?

'You might well look surprised,' the other woman continued. 'I suppose you didn't reckon on me finding out what you've been up to.'

Shari darted a stricken glance at Griff. Surely he wouldn't just sit there and let her take the blame? Weak as she had been in submitting to his lovemaking, she hadn't initiated it. But he was looking totally unconcerned and as he dismounted, he enquired coolly,

'What's all this about, Estelle? For goodness' sake save the reproaches and accusations until we know what you're talking about.'

'I'm not reproaching *you*, darling! You'll be as horrified and as furious as *I* am, when I tell you what that girl has been up to.'

Shari went limp in the saddle with relief. Whatever it was, it had no connection with Griff's behaviour towards her, or hers towards him. Then she noticed that Estelle clutched a long, official-looking envelope.

'Read that!'

Griff did so, taking his time.

'Then they've turned down your application,' he said at last, a strange note in his voice. 'So that's that then.'

'You mean . . . the application to turn Threlkeld into a holiday centre?' Shari had to ask, her voice eager.

'As if you didn't know.' Estelle snatched the letter from Griff's hand, stabbing at it with one red-tipped nail. 'You see this? "Taking into consideration the weight of public feeling . . . the petition submitted to us." Well, I've seen that petition and guess whose name headed the list?' The finger was turned on Shari. 'Your young friend here. I've tried my darnedest to overcome her ridiculous hostility. Against my better judgment, I agreed to her working for you, but she hasn't even any loyalty to *you*, and you've been stupid enough to think she might.'

'Estelle, that'll do!' Griff interrupted.

As for Shari, she knew her mouth must have fallen open in surprise. She'd signed no petition. She'd known of its existence, but no one had approached her for her support. Whoever was organising it must have considered it tactless to do so, since the sale of Threlkeld and her grandmother's finances must depend on the results of the planning application.

'I didn't . . .' She began her denial, but Estelle cut across her words.

'You've been against me and my ideas right from the beginning. I can understand you not wanting to lose your home, and so I tried to make allowances, but this is too much. It's obvious that you engineered the whole thing. You needn't think you've won, though. I don't give up that easily. I shall appeal.'

'Do you really think it's worth all the bother?' Griff asked quietly.

Shari looked at him, puzzled. She had expected anger from him too at the frustration of the plans he and Estelle shared. Did he believe, as Estelle did, that *she* had been responsible for the petition?

'Rub Conker down for me, will you?' Griff's voice broke across her thoughts as he spoke to Jimmy. 'I'd do it myself, but I think Estelle and I have to talk about this development.' He thrust the reins into the younger man's hands and steered Estelle away, his hand at her elbow supporting her across the cobbles, his blond head bent attentively to listen to her words. He hadn't even spared her a final glance, Shari thought miserably, hadn't even given her a chance to defend herself.

'I didn't start that petition, you know,' she told Jimmy, a slight break in her voice, as they unsaddled. 'And I didn't sign it either!'

'I know.' His voice was low, his head lowered over his task, but she could see a tell-tale flushed cheek.

'*Jimmy!*' she said accusingly.

He turned to face her then.

'I didn't start it either, Shari. You don't think I'd have stood here and let you take the blame? I don't know who did, but I did sign it, on your behalf, because I thought I knew how you felt about the whole thing; and I thought whoever had started it wouldn't dare to ask you, so . . .'

'Where did you sign it? If my name was at the top of the list, you must know who started it?'

'No, there were lists everywhere, at the pub, at the back of the church, in the shop. It was just bad luck that the one I signed was put at the front. He paused, then, 'Shari, I would have owned up just now, but I don't want to lose this job. Gran's been on at me about staying in Beckdale at least as long as she's alive.'

'She could live to be ninety,' Shari pointed out.

'I don't think so.' He sounded sad. 'Do you remember what we were saying about uprooting old people. Haven't you noticed? She's been getting awfully frail lately. She's holding on, I know, until the Hall is sold and she can move into a cottage with Mrs Freeman, but somehow I don't think she'll last long after that. I think all the upheaval will finish her.' He hesitated. 'You may as well face it, it could finish *both* of them.'

'And that will be *their* fault too!' Shari was almost as fond of Lily as she was of Abigail Freeman and the thought that she might lose them both, that Jimmy might lose his grandmother. . .

'Not really. Be fair! Your Gran had to sell. Somebody had to buy. If it hadn't been Miss Garner and Mr Masterson, it would have been someone else.'

'I know!' she admitted. The words came out on a sob, but she had to be honest. It wasn't Estelle's fault that Threlkeld had fallen on hard times. It wasn't Griff's fault, but she badly needed a reason to stop loving Griff. If only she could have believed her own words! All she could do was save her pride by hiding that love, until she could get away.

CHAPTER SEVEN

SHE was managing pretty well, she assured herself repeatedly in the weeks that followed. Some of her success was due to the iron determination that had always formed a part of her character, her refusal when alone to allow her thoughts to dwell on him. But she was busy too. August *was* a busy month, with all the local events to look forward to, sports meetings, sheepdog trials, but chiefly the Ramsdale Agricultural Show. She was determined that Rainbow and Jet should acquit themselves well in their event. Her hopes were high for Jimmy too. He was entering Spectre for the hound trail, run in conjunction with the show.

What Shari did not realise was just how much strain she was imposing upon herself by this unnatural self-control, strain that fined down her already slender figure and shadowed the violet eyes.

The day before the Show, she spent most of her time in the tack-room, cleaning and polishing until everything shone like new. Griff had entered Conker for a couple of events and she had half feared that he would be working alongside her, but he had seemed almost uninterested, saying that he had a business appointment in the next valley and delegating the task to Jimmy.

'He might as well let you ride him too, for all the interest he's showing,' she grumbled.

'That upsets you, doesn't it?' Jimmy said perceptively. 'You'd rather *he* was here, doing this. You still feel the same way about him, don't you?'

At first she denied it, but she knew he wasn't deceived.

'All right! But I'll get over it, you'll see. I have to! He belongs to Estelle.'

She had reiterated this statement so often that now Jimmy didn't question its accuracy.

'And I suppose if all her schemes fall through, *he'll* be leaving too, taking his animals with him.'

Shock took Shari by the throat, making her unable to speak for a moment. She should have thought of that for herself. She ought to be rejoicing at the possibility. If Estelle and Griff left, her quiet little world would go back to normal, *she* would return to normal. Oh, to hell with it! She threw down her polishing cloth. Who was she trying to fool? She could never return to the past any more than Threlkeld itself could. Hall and farm had to be sold for the sake of her grandmother's health and peace of mind and if Griff and Estelle left, the whole dreary business would have to be gone through again; and she'd rather have Griff living there than a complete stranger. Even if it meant he'd be living there with Estelle. She wanted Griff to be happy and if Estelle and Threlkeld had the power to bestow that happiness, she must wish it for him.

'Then I hope the appeal succeeds,' she said, surprising Jimmy, then, irritably, 'Oh, come on, we've done enough work on tack. We've got three horses to groom, then I'm having an early night. It's no use plaiting manes and bandaging until the morning.'

The day of the Agricultural Show, Shari and the whole of Lakeland awoke to an uncertain start. It had rained overnight and there was still a possibility of wet weather. But, looking towards the mountains, Shari could see that no obstinate, slate-grey clouds hung over them. But whatever the weather, with their usual optimism, stall holders would now be setting out their displays.

By the time they were ready to set out, the skies had

lightened; there was even increasing warmth in the sun. Ramsdale Valley was a seething hive of activity, with crowds streaming towards the showground. The field itself was packed with cattle, sheep, horses and dogs, and folk, there determined to enjoy themselves. Along one side of the area were ranged the cattle, milkers, their udders pristinely clean, gleaming heifers, nervous calves, wearing too, in some cases, the red white or blue rosettes of success on their foreheads. There were powerful bulls too, chained to the fence by their nose rings. Farmers swarmed around the sheep pens, comparing the virtues of Herdwick, Swaledale and other breeds. Bookmakers collected bets for the hound trail. Huge agricultural horses, bright with garlands, stood placidly waiting for their turn in the show-ring and the whole place resounded to the excited chatter of small boys and girls on ponies.

Shari had tried to hide her chagrin at finding that Estelle intended to accompany Griff to the Show. She wouldn't have expected the other woman to demonstrate any interest in an event concerned mainly with animals, which she professed to dislike. Maybe Estelle had decided it would be wise to start playing the part of a farmer's future wife. Oh, how she hoped Estelle *would* make him happy. That was all that really mattered. She believed she could cope with her own heartache if she thought that was the case.

As she made her way back towards the horseboxes, she caught a glimpse of Estelle just leaving the area, talking to a short, squat man in riding breeches. There was no mistaking the svelte, voluptuous figure, incongruous in a smart skirt suit and new, bright red wellingtons. She must have mislaid Griff. It was only a fleeting source of satisfaction. Lucky Estelle, who could spend the rest of her life with him.

It was time to take the horses to the collecting ring. There was still no sign of Griff, who also intended to ride in this class, and she couldn't possibly lead three horses, she thought crossly. Oh well, if he missed his turn it would be his own fault. But as she led her own mounts away he came hurrying up to collect Conker and he was only a few yards behind her as she reached the ringside. But she didn't turn her head or wait for him.

There were several entrants ahead of Shari. She was to ride Rainbow first. She was glad of this; the mare was a steady, sensible little beast and almost certain to get a clear round, which would do much to settle her owner's nerves.

It was encouraging too, to see that neither of the first two entrants had made a clear round. The first girl had allowed her mount to take off too soon, with the result that a pole came off and horse and rider went flying. The second contestant's mount had stopped dead at the water jump, his rider landing with an almighty splash much appreciated by the spectators.

A sudden frisson along her nerves told Shari that Griff was right behind her. She didn't have to see him or hear his voice to know it. She would be aware of his presence, she thought, even if she were suddenly struck blind and deaf.

'Good luck, Shari!'

'Thanks!' she said gruffly and knew it sounded more ungracious than she'd intended. She looked up at him meaning to say more, but the expression on his face froze the words on her lips. Though it was only early in the day, he looked utterly weary and somehow defeated. Then her number was called and she mounted swiftly, telling herself sternly that Griff's appearance was no concern of hers, that she must concentrate on the task in hand.

Rainbow was moving sweetly, measuring her stride and taking off in the right area every time, nice, neat jumps, knees up and forward, feet tucked up and away.

Incredibly it was over; they had gone clear, the first clear round of the class. There would be jealousy among the other competitors, old rivals, but who cared? Shari rode from the ring to loud applause.

Griff's number followed immediately after hers and they passed, only inches apart; but he did not even look in her direction and she was sure he didn't hear the 'good luck' that she murmured. But she had to watch him. Estelle was there too, she noticed for the first time, still with the small, squat man. Of course Estelle would want to see Griff compete.

Once Shari knew he had gone clear she moved away to change horses, for soon it would be Jet's turn to show her paces.

From the moment she rode the black mare into the collecting ring, she felt that there was something wrong. Jet was moving obediently, quietly, too quietly. She had none of her usual sparkle. It was almost as if the mare were tired; but she couldn't be. Shari had been careful only to give her light exercise the previous day.

She cantered Jet in the preliminary circle, before approaching the first jump, but it was a reluctant canter, the action dull and heavy like that of an old horse. The first jump was always a low one, but the moment Jet approached it she began acting up, side-stepping, unresponsive to Shari's urging. The mare refused! Jet, who usually took everything with grasshopper-like insouciance! Setting her lips, Shari made her approach the jump a second time, with the same result and at the third refusal she was disqualified.

Shari was more bewildered than chagrined at Jet's behaviour. It was so uncharacteristic, as was the way she was plodding out of the ring now, head drooping, the picture of dejection. She must be sick.

Griff and Estelle were waiting for her.

'What went wrong?'

Shari shook her head, but Estelle was ready with an answer.

'My dear,' she said wearily, 'after all this time, surely the penny must have dropped. Shari's enmity towards us. Isn't it obvious? She couldn't have been trying. She'd hardly want *your* mare to outjump hers; and if it had come to a jump-off, that would almost certainly have been the case.'

Shari couldn't blame Estelle for her suspicion, or for voicing it. It was justified retaliation for some of the things *she* had said about and to Estelle. What was the use of making fervent denials? In a choice between the two of them, Griff would be bound to believe Estelle. She dismounted and led Jet back to the box where Rainbow was tethered, awaiting her next appearance. The nearest horsebox was just being loaded, with the mount of a rather superior young man Shari had encountered once or twice before. This youth looked at Shari contemptuously and, she thought, smugly.

'Didn't do so well with that one, did you?' he jeered. 'Obvious your family doesn't know much about horses.'

'My family?' What had her family to do with anything? Abigail Freeman was here, but seated in the only stand, out of deference to her age and frailty. Shari doubted if this young man even knew her grandmother.

'Well, your family or your friends,' the teenager amended. 'I thought she was your sister. Tall girl, older than you, with red hair. Stuck-up piece.'

The description of red hair, the manner, brought Estelle to mind.

'She's no relation, or friend,' she said shortly, 'but what about her?'

'I thought she was just a fool, but if you say she's no friend of yours that explains it, giving a horse a full bucket of water just before it's got to jump.' He closed up the back of the horse box and moved round towards the passenger seat.

'Wait!' Shari cried. 'Don't go. Would you be prepared to repeat what you've just said to the horse's owner?'

'Not on your life. I'm not getting involved in your local feuds. I'm in a hurry anyway. I've got another event today, at Kendal.'

'Please,' she began, but it was no use. The engine was already revving, the cab door slammed shut and the horsebox began to move slowly away over the rutted ground. She stood and watched it go. Probably it wouldn't have been any use to have the lad repeat his words.

With a start, she realised she should have been in the collecting-ring again, ages ago, for the jump-off; and, as she anticipated, she was too late. She hadn't been there to respond when her number was called; the event was over.

'What happened to you?' Estelle asked. 'Did you lose your nerve?'

Shari bit hard on her lip. She longed to accuse Estelle. If she ever got a chance to prove what the other woman had done, just let her watch out.

Back at Threlkeld, the horsebox unloaded, Griff dismissed Jimmy with a peremptory command, leading the horses into their stalls himself.

With shaking hands, Shari fed Rainbow, then performed the same office for Jet, who seemed livelier now, almost recovered from the deliberate sabotage.

'Well, Shari, what's *your* explanation of this afternoon? I presume you have one?' With no nerves to unsteady him, he had already attended to Conker and now he was in Jet's stall, which seemed very crowded, the mare, herself and Griff's tall form.

She made no answer, though the words boiled in her mind and he began to examine the animal, running knowledgeable hands over it.

'There's nothing wrong with this mare,' he stated at last, his tone astringent.

'No,' she agreed, 'there isn't now.'

'But there was this afternoon?'

'Yes.'

'Then what the hell was it? What did you do to her?'

'Do to her? *Me?*' Shari's voice rose protestingly. 'It had nothing to do with me.' She edged her way out of the box, going into the tack room. He followed her.

'Convince me!'

'Oh, don't be a fool,' she snapped, rounding on him. 'I've been schooling her for weeks, looking forward to riding her. She could have won that class hands down, even against your horse.'

'And Rainbow?' he persisted. So Estelle's poisonous words had been effective.

'Rainbow went clear the first time, but with Conker and Jet competing the fences would have got higher. She's only a pony, Jet can give her two hands.' She reached for cleaning materials.

'Leave that!' he ordered. 'Are you telling me you wouldn't have minded your own mare being beaten?'

'If I was riding the winner anyway? Don't be stupid!' Again she tried to begin work, but he snatched the cloths from her hands.

'Leave that! I want to get to the bottom of this. So what went wrong?'

'Sabotage.' She said it unwillingly, knowing he wouldn't be content to leave the matter there.

He looked at her for a while, the blue eyes intent, but she held his gaze without faltering; she had nothing with which to reproach herself.

'Who? Why? And how?'

She ignored the first question. He wouldn't believe her anyhow.

'To discredit me maybe, perhaps to settle a grudge. The method was simple. A bucket of water half an hour before the class.'

Griff swore roundly, the only time she had ever heard

him use more than a single expletive. Then his eyes narrowed.

'You're forgetting something. I asked you who?'

She set her lips, shaking her head.

'Don't try to tell me you don't know. If you know so much you must know that too.'

'All right, I do know, but I'm not going to make any accusations.'

Until now his annoyance had been well under control, but not any more. He moved until he was standing over her, not touching her, but he might as well have been.

'Who are you protecting?' His voice lashed at her.

'No one.' As if she would protect Estelle! If she only had an iota of proof!

'Then I can only think of one person. Jimmy.'

'No!' she cried out. 'Jimmy wouldn't! And anyhow, he wasn't anywhere near the horses. He was with Charlie Garner all afternoon, watching the hound trails. He won some money. Ask Charlie if you don't believe me.'

'I don't intend to waste my time asking around, when you know the answer, and I intend to have it out of you, Shari, even if we have to stay here all night.'

Since he was between her and any means of escape, this was no idle threat and the thought of what a few hours confined here with him might do to her resolution to dislike him, forget about him, made her blurt out the information he demanded.

'O.K. But I'm only telling you because the thought of being stuck in here with you sickens me!'

For an instant a gleam of mockery showed in the sapphire-blue eyes.

'Really? Well, we won't go into that just now, another time perhaps. The culprit's name, if you please!'

'You won't believe me,' she pleaded desperately.

'Try me,' he suggested.

'It was Estelle.'

'Estelle? Estelle who wouldn't go near a horse, wouldn't know which end to offer the bucket to.' Disbelief she had expected, but was he daring to laugh at her too?

'Yes, your precious girlfriend,' she snapped. 'Oh, she may dislike horses, she may even be scared of them, but it doesn't call for much courage to stick a bucket within easy reach of a tethered animal. But of course *you* wouldn't hear a word against her, would you? But you'd believe her accusation against me.'

She wasn't sure what she expected now. What she did *not* expect was a laugh which seemed to stem from real amusement, a laugh whose sound carried to her ears long after he had turned and walked away towards the house. Why was he so amused? What was there to laugh at? And at whom was he laughing? If he was laughing at *her* . . .

Suddenly furious, she marched after him. She was just in time to see him enter her grandmother's private parlour, closing the door firmly behind him. He hadn't believed her; he'd been laughing at what he imagined to be her pitiful attempt to excuse herself, or Jimmy. Now he'd gone to complain to her grandmother. Oh, how could he? He knew her grandmother mustn't be upset. And it was no good her bursting in there and attempting to contradict him, that would only upset Abigail Freeman even more. But there was something she *could* do.

She tiptoed the rest of the way to the parlour door and listened intently, to no avail. The timbers of Threlkeld Hall were thick and sturdy; all she could hear was a low rumble of sound, punctuated by . . . more laughter? Griff's deep-throated, her grandmother's high, light and amused.

Mystified, but nonetheless a little relieved that there

did not seem to be conflict taking place behind the parlour door, she moved on and upstairs to her own room.

Changing her riding gear for jeans and shirt, Shari experienced a sudden feeling of flatness. It was in part, she knew, reaction to the unpleasantness over Jet, and in particular to the tensions of the last few moments. But it was more than that. There was nothing to which she could look forward. The Show had ended on a low note, an unusual occurrence. In other years she had returned home with at least two rosettes to her credit and, in a mood to celebrate, she and Jimmy had always gone back to Ramsdale in the evening for the barn dance, in the open if fine, under canvas if the weather turned treacherous.

This year, she was surprised and a little chagrined that Jimmy hadn't suggested that they follow their usual routine. Still, there was nothing to celebrate this year, quite the reverse. Yet she felt restless. This seemed such a tame ending to one of the biggest local events of the year and the hours until bedtime loomed heavily before her, boring and empty.

It was ironic, she thought, leaning on the wide sill of her bedroom window, her eyes fixed on the mountain tops, that tonight should promise to be a fine dry one, ideal weather for the dance.

'You look rather like Juliet, waiting for Romeo!' A deep voice at ground level made her start and glance down. Griff was standing beneath her window, legs straddled, hands in pockets, his blond head tilted backwards, as he gazed up at her. The very masculine stance had a powerful effect on her pulse rate. He might not be the handsomest man she'd ever seen, but he certainly was the most compellingly attractive. 'I thought you'd be busy beautifying yourself,' he continued.

'What for?' she asked flatly. In her already

jaundiced state of mind, his words seemed to imply that he found her present appearance drab and uninteresting.

'The barn dance, of course. Your grandmother tells me it's traditional after the show, at least for everyone sound in wind and limb!'

'Oh that! I'm not going this year.' She began to move away from the window. But his words halted her.

'Why? Has Romeo let you down?'

'Romeo?' she puzzled.

'Jimmy, of course. Isn't he your "best friend"? You keep telling me so! Of course, if you'd like a substitute partner, I just happen to be at a loose end myself,' he volunteered. Did he feel sorry for her, because she'd been such an abysmal failure today, and what made him think she'd accept?

'I'm not bothered about going this time,' she repeated, 'the atmosphere won't be the same as other years.'

'Oh? How's that? Because you're not the "Victor Ludorum" this year? Because you can't take being beaten?'

'No, of course not.'

'People will think that's what it is,' he stated with hateful certainty. 'You wouldn't want to be branded a bad loser, would you?' Since she didn't answer, he added persuasively, 'Let *me* take you to the dance, you haven't a partner, and neither have I. We'll console each other.'

What had happened to Estelle then? Frostily, she asked him.

'Oh, she's got other fish to fry tonight. She's talking business with her stepfather. Didn't you see him with her at the Show?'

So the stumpy little man had been Charlie Garner's brother. He wasn't a patch on Charlie for looks.

'Well, are you coming?' Griff said impatiently. 'If we

don't get started soon, we'll miss several dances and I feel in a dancing mood.'

Suddenly so did Shari and temptation, inclination, warred with the instinct which told her it would be safer to refuse.

'I haven't anything suitable to wear,' she temporised.

'What did you wear last year?'

'Oh, jeans and a T-shirt. It's not a very formal affair and Jimmy doesn't care what I . . .' Too late, she stopped. What she had been going to say did not tie in with the image of a caring relationship she had tried to create.

'Doesn't mind what you look like? Of course not! Sensible chap. I would have thought less of him if he did. Why should he mind? Why should I? It's the person inside the clothes, not the clothes themselves that matter. Now, make up your mind, yes or no?'

No, she thought, but, 'Yes' she said, quickly, breathlessly. She was an idiot. She was only letting herself in for more heartbreak; but it would be better than moping up here all alone, and that horrible sensation of flatness had vanished, leaving her instead excited and tremulous. But still she hesitated.

'I don't know why you should ask me. I didn't think you were very pleased with me at the moment.'

'I can't go on my own,' he pointed out.

'Rubbish,' she said vehemently, because he hadn't denied his displeasure. 'There'll be any number of unattached girls there, only too happy to . . .' She stopped, confused.

'To what?' He sounded amused, confident of her answer.

She'd been going to say 'only too happy to see an unattached, attractive male.' but that savoured too much of a compliment. Instead, she changed it to,

'Well, anyway, there'll be plenty of girls without partners and after this afternoon, I shouldn't think you'd want my company.'

'Shari!' he said firmly. 'Let's get one thing straight. I don't blame you for what happened to Jet, if that's what's worrying you.' It was.

'But you don't think it was Estelle either?' She held her breath, but his tone was just as certain.

'No, I *know* it couldn't have been Estelle. Now could we stop this pointless conversation? I'm getting a crick in my neck! I'll give you fifteen minutes. Since you're not a great one for powder and paint that should be ample, and then if you're not down here, I'll come up and get you!'

She wouldn't need fifteen minutes, Shari thought wryly, regarding her image in the mirror. It was only a matter of substituting a more respectable pair of jeans for the faded and frayed pair she already wore. She'd never felt the lack of party clothes, or even an ordinary dress before. But now she found herself regretting that just for one magical night, the memories of which might have to last her a lifetime, she couldn't appear feminine and desirable.

A tap on the door had her glancing nervously at her wristwatch. Surely she hadn't been daydreaming that long? The time Griff had allowed her wasn't up already? But his knock would have been noisier, more peremptory. It was Abigail Freeman who entered the room, breathing a little heavily from her unaccustomed climb of the stairs. Since her illness, she had slept in a downstairs bedroom.

'Griff tells me you're going to the dance with him.' Abigail seemed inordinately pleased and Shari nodded warily. 'And knowing you, you haven't a rag to wear.' The times Abigail had tried to persuade her granddaughter to buy dresses, even if only in case of a special occasion. Now Abigail couldn't regret Shari's adamant refusals any more than Shari did herself. 'Here, try this on and be quick.' She smiled, as she added: 'I understand you haven't much time.' Then, 'Well, what are you waiting for?' as Shari stared incredulously at the lengths of material draped over her grandmother's arm.

'But what? Where?' Shari asked confusedly, as automatically obedient, she began to unzip her jeans, peel off her shirt.

'Your mother left these behind,' Abigail told her wryly, 'when she went off in such a hurry all those years ago. They're probably hopelessly outdated and probably quite unsuitable for a barn dance. I wouldn't know, but at least they'll fit you. Fortunately, Elizabeth was small and slight too. The dress has its own underskirt and I think these shoes will do. If not you'll just have to suffer. Let us be beautiful or die!' she declaimed.

With mounting excitement, for she had never seen, let alone worn anything half as lovely, Shari slipped the dress over her head and her feet into the high-heeled shoes. Her grandmother was right. They were a little on the tight side. Shari's feet were more accustomed to pumps or fell boots. But for tonight she would endure anything, if she could only be beautiful in Griff's eyes.

She turned towards the long mirror, which normally she only accorded the most cursory of glances. Tonight she stood so still that the cheval glass might have been a frame, setting off the picture of a vision of unexpected loveliness. The dress had transformed her from an appealing, gamine-like tomboy into the very essence of womanhood, a fragile, ethereal creature, who could not possibly, by any stretch of the imagination, have bestridden a horse, or tramped endless miles of rugged fell country.

It was a floating, filmy dream of a dress, in a blend of oriental colours which age had subtly muted and faded. The hemline was deliberately uneven, elf-like, and there were split, drifting sleeves. From the neckline Shari's grave, oval face and dark cloud of hair rose like those of some fey, faery princess.

'It's incredible,' Abigail Freeman said with satisfaction, 'what clothes can do for a woman. This is how I've always wanted you to look!'

Excitement, the thrilled anticipation of wondering what Griff would think when he saw her, brought a light-hearted giggle to Shari's lips.

'Not very practical though, Gran, for haymaking and mucking out stables.'

But Abigail was in a brisk, no-nonsense mood.

'That dress needs make-up to set it off,' she declared. 'You've a good healthy colour, thank heaven, and a clear complexion, so you don't need paint and powder, but you most certainly do need eye make-up and lipstick.'

'I don't possess any,' Shari said, 'and anyway, I'd feel very uncomfortable with my eyes and mouth all gummed up.'

'Don't exaggerate!' her grandmother commanded. 'Wait there!'

Her footsteps faded away along the landing and soon there was the sound of low-voiced consultation and when the door opened again, Shari turned from rapt contemplation of this new self to see Estelle advancing upon her, a small, compact vanity case in her hand.

'Sit down, quickly,' the other woman directed, 'your grandmother tells me we haven't much time.'

Too stunned to protest, though her brain was teeming with questions, Shari found herself seated at her dressing-table, *obeying Estelle!* Closing her eyes, whilst the other woman applied deft, delicate touches of colour to eye and brow areas, parting and stretching her lips for the palest of pink lipsticks.

Able to speak at least, Shari regarded Estelle's reflection in the mirror.

'Why?' she asked. 'Why are you doing this? Why should you?'

'Mrs Freeman said you were going dancing with

Griff.' Estelle's reply was calm, matter-of-fact. 'She said you'd never used make-up before and asked if I'd help.'

'And you don't *mind*?' Shari was still bewildered, incredulous. 'You don't mind that *I'm* going out with Griff?'

'Of course not. Why should I?' the other responded briskly. 'That's his business, and yours. Now, a little spray of scent and that should do it and only just in time. I think your partner's getting impatient!' Sure enough, just below the window, a voice was calling Shari's name.

Still in a daze of unbelief, Shari rose and pulled a soft, matching stole around her shoulders, which, she realised with a sudden blush, were almost as bare as if she were in her bikini. But somehow, in a dress, it seemed more daring to expose all this flesh. Still she hesitated.

'Estelle?' she almost pleaded. 'I don't understand, after all I've done. Why should you be so . . . so kind to me?'

'Nonsense!' Estelle laughed, but she seemed pleased by Shari's half-apology. 'Go on, hurry up now.'

'Thank you, Estelle. Thank you very much,' Shari heard herself saying.

Slowly she left her room and went towards the head of the staircase. To her mind, there was only one logical explanation. Estelle didn't mind Griff escorting her because she herself was otherwise engaged that evening, and because she was totally sure of him, of his loyalty.

On the top step Shari hesitated, about to turn back, to refuse to go. But it was too late. Griff was in the hallway, taking the stairs two at a time, capturing her hands, holding them aloft, the better to admire her. He whistled appreciatively, through his teeth.

'I *like* your idea of jeans and T-shirt!' he said, the

wide gap-toothed smile illuminating his bronzed face; and somehow she knew his admiration was genuine, that for once he wasn't teasing. The light in the sapphire-blue eyes was not one of mockery this time, but of awe. 'I never dreamt "my stable lad" was capable of such a transformation. Must I have you home before midnight? In case all your finery vanishes?'

She couldn't help laughing, all doubts and fears temporarily suspended. She *did* feel a little like Cinderella transformed into a princess. Just for tonight, until the witching hour of midnight, when she became Cinderella again, Griff was hers. Then she must firmly put all thoughts of him aside. She had been called for another interview next week; perhaps, she thought with a heavy heart, this time she would be lucky.

All the paraphernalia of Showday had been cleared away except for the large marquee, and now it was possible to see how the long, green field sloped down towards the lake. Already, in the evening sunlight, moving gracefully to the music of fiddlers, groups of people were dancing to well-loved tunes.

The dances were lively and boisterous, the 'Cumberland Square Eight', 'When Three Meet', the 'Virginia Reel' and many more, dances where there was only the briefest contact between partners and little or no time for prolonged conversations. As Griff had said, only the elderly and infirm were absent and in particular all the horsey fraternity had returned for the evening festivities, including the youth who had sneered over Jet's failure in the arena.

'How did you get on at Kendal?' Shari asked him, as a progressive Barn Dance made them partners for a while.

'Two firsts and a third,' he said airily, 'and against better competition than I had here. Did you give your "friend" what for,' the youth enquired, 'watering your mare just before her event?'

'No,' Shari said flatly and the sandy eyebrows lifted enquiringly.

'No? You and your boyfriend must be a bit soft.'

'My boyfriend?'

'Well, the chap you arrived with. I assumed he was the boyfriend? Look, he's dancing with her now, matey as you like, or didn't you tell him?'

Estelle was here? Shari glanced over her shoulder, then stiffened, missing her step. The redhead dancing with Griff wasn't Estelle. She was an old jumping rival, the girl whose mount had landed her in the water that afternoon. A lot of things suddenly became clear to Shari and she was mortified to think how she had wrongly accused Estelle. It was a wonder Griff was even speaking to her, let alone escorting her to this dance. *He'd* maintained Estelle's innocence all along and he'd been right.

'No, my friend doesn't know anything about that girl,' she told her partner and then to her relief, the dance separated them. But not before the youth's words drifted back,

'And aren't you going to tackle her?'

'No,' she called back, 'not worth it!'

And it didn't seem worth creating a fuss. Shari had deeper problems on her mind, not least being that she must admit her error to Griff and apologise to Estelle. Even though she hadn't accused the other woman to her face, Griff might well have mentioned her suspicions; and anyway, Shari knew she couldn't live with herself with a conscience ill at ease.

As the evening wore on the dances became less energetic, the musicians playing slower, dreamier tunes.

'Just right for a waltz,' Griff told Shari, holding out his hand to her.

A waltz? It would mean him putting his arms around her; a quivering half-longing, half-dread possessed her at the thought and as he moved in on her, she had to

bite her lip to prevent a betraying cry of protest
escaping her lips; as it was, she murmured faintly,

'I'm not very good at this sort of dancing. I don't
think I...'

'Oh yes you can, pint-size!' His voice was softly
compelling. 'You'd be surprised what you can do if you
try.'

As he held her close, as she'd known it would, the
familiar, trembling, aching feeling spread through the
pit of her stomach; and her heart beat extra fast, as
deafening to her own ears as the beat of a drum. His
thumb was absently, as if unaware of what he was
doing, stroking the nape of her neck.

Body rigid, her tongue cleaving to the roof of her
mouth, she endured their closeness. Though their steps
were slow, her head was reeling, as if they still
performed the fast, intricate gyrations of the country
dances. She felt an almost overwhelming desire to close
her eyes, lean her head forward against his shoulder, let
her lips brush against the sinewy cord of his neck, to
feel the steady pulse of the blood through his veins. But
somehow she resisted the impulse. Her tension
communicated itself to him for,

'Relax, Shari,' he murmured, 'it's only a dance.'

But it wasn't, not to her. She felt as if everyone were
watching them, that everyone must know exactly how
she felt about the man who held her, whose body was
so disturbing to hers. She realised now the extent of her
former naivety, until he had made her aware for the
first time in her life of her body's needs. A long quiver
ran through her and as though it triggered off some
responsive nerve in him, he hauled her even closer.

Shari swallowed convulsively. She couldn't think of
any place she'd rather be right now than here, clasped
closely in Griff's arms. His cheek, somehow, seemed to
have come to rest against her hair, his breath fanning
warmly, deliciously over her temple; and their steps had

slowed, to the point where they were barely moving. It
was heaven on earth, but it shouldn't be happening.
Estelle had sent them off together, trustingly; and Shari
found that though she still envied the other woman, still
could not like the idea of a new mistress at Threlkeld, she
couldn't deliberately betray Estelle's trust, especially
since her discovery this evening that she had misjudged her.

'Griff,' she managed to articulate his name, 'I'm . . .
I'm sorry!'

'For what?' he murmured deep throatedly against
her ear, making it even more difficult for her to speak.

'For what I said about Estelle, about Jet. It wasn't
her.'

'I know that,' he said comfortably. 'Estelle was with
her stepfather all afternoon, talking business with a
farmer from over Grasmere way, and apart from
having no opportunity, she wouldn't dream of injuring
one of my horses. We've known each other since we
were children and we've always been the best of friends,
with no secrets from each other.'

'I shall apologise to Estelle, of course,' she said.

'No need. She doesn't know of your suspicions. I
certainly wasn't going to tell her.'

Was that because Griff hadn't wanted to cause
trouble, because he hadn't wanted to hurt Estelle? He
hadn't loosened his grasp of her at all; and suddenly she
felt she could bear it no longer. Her nerves were at
screaming-point and she felt perilously close to tears.
Her admission hadn't served any purpose. He'd never
believed her allegations against Estelle anyway and her
acknowledgement of the wrong she'd done the other
woman hadn't made her feel any better. In fact she felt
worse. She should never have come tonight. She should
have had more pride. Abruptly she tried to pull free.

'I'd like to go home now,' she said through clenched
teeth that only just prevented a sob from escaping. As it
was she felt sure he must be aware of the irregularity of

the breaths she had been drawing for some minutes.

'O.K. Why not?' He accepted her statement and steered her out of the crowd of dancers. 'It's getting late and we have things to talk about.'

'We do?' In her surprise her tension relaxed a little, and she did not shrug away from the arm about her shoulders that steered her back to the place where they had parked the car.

'What do we have to talk about?' Shari asked tremulously, as they drove away from Ramsdale. He'd decided he didn't want her to work for him after all. She *knew* it. Oh, Shari couldn't blame him if he dismissed her. For the moment she'd quite forgotten that she intended to leave anyway, and apprehension gripped her, clenching her stomach muscles, drying her mouth, closing up her throat.

'You haven't heard a word I've said,' Griff accused and she realised that while she'd been waiting for the blow to fall, he'd been talking quietly, conversationally; about what she had no idea. 'I said,' he repeated himself, 'if you could wish for anything, absolutely anything in the whole world, what would it be?'

She didn't have to consider. The answer had been indelibly engraved upon her heart for some time now. Above all else she would like to spend the rest of her life with Griff, as his wife. But it was impossible to speak the truth and she had to pretend to study his question. Again it wasn't too hard, her second choice.

'That Threlkeld didn't have to be sold, that Gran and I could stay on there always.'

'You still hate the idea of Estelle owning it then?' he said drily and she thought there was a note of disappointment in his voice.

'No.' Now was her chance to make amends. 'No, I don't mind quite as much as I did. She's not such a bad sort after all. I guess I was just ...' She'd nearly said 'jealous', but bit back the word in time.

The car had stopped, she realised. Griff had run it off the road on to a grass verge and now he turned sideways in his seat to consider her shadowy profile. His arm moved and she started, but he was merely reaching up to flick on the overhead light. Still she darted an uneasy glance at him. It was too cosy, too companionable here in the bright interior, which had suddenly cut both of them off from the dark world outside, enclosing them in a small, intimate cocoon in which nothing existed but themselves.

'At least it's nice to know you don't dislike Estelle as much as you did and perhaps I can remove your last motive for doing so. She isn't going to buy Threlkeld.'

Mixed feelings flooded Shari's being, relief initially, because Threlkeld wouldn't be converted into some hideous holiday centre. But dismay quickly followed. This latest news would just mean more worry and stress for her grandmother.

'Nothing to say?' Griff enquired.

'I suppose her appeal against the planning refusal was turned down. I'm sorry! Gran will be disappointed.'

'It's nice to hear you say so. I believe little Shari is growing up at last.' His voice was amused, but heart-tuggingly caressive. 'But no, we've heard nothing further about the appeal. Estelle's been offered the chance of a larger place over towards Grasmere, with more hope of being able to carry out her plans and she prefers the area anyway. It's less isolated. Her stepfather came up and looked it over and as her financial adviser, I could only agree. It has better prospects.'

'*Well, that's charming!*' Shari couldn't hold in the indignant explosion. 'Letting poor Gran down at the eleventh hour!' This would mean a change in Griff's plans. He would be transferring his ideas, his scheme for breeding ponies, for pony-trekking, to Estelle's new

site in Grasmere. She hoped desperately that he wasn't
going to follow up this information by asking her again
to reconsider her decision to leave. Hoped he wasn't
going to ask her to go and work for him at Grasmere,
because she would have to refuse and it was going to
take all her courage and willpower to prevent herself
from bursting into tears.

She'd decided to go right away, once her grandmother
was safely established in her cottage, put as many miles
as possible between herself and Griff. Her interview
next week was with a riding-stables in the depth of
Wales; if she were to obtain the position, she planned to
visit Abigail only once she was sure she could risk an
encounter with Griff, even if she had to explain to her
grandmother the reason for her infrequent returns to
the valley. Abigail would never betray such a
confidence and the confession would spare her
grandmother the hurt of believing Shari was callously
neglecting her. But if Threlkeld remained unsold, she
would *have* to stay on with Abigail, see her through the
wearisome business of finding another buyer; and
knowing that only a range or two of mountains divided
her from a place where Griff and Estelle would be
happily establishing their life together.

'No one's letting Mrs Freeman down.' Griff's deep
voice cut through the fog of mounting pain. '*I'm* going
to buy Threlkeld for myself.'

Shari was too taken aback at first to be able to
comment. It sounded such an odd arrangement, two
separate establishments. But then, of course, he and
Estelle had always planned to buy more than one
property. That was why they had stayed on for such a
long period, paying for their accommodation. She
supposed Griff could easily live at Grasmere and put in
a manager at Threlkeld, commute between the two.

'So, subject to certain conditions, there's no reason at
all why you and your grandmother should ever leave.'

He was going to ask *her* to be his caretaker? Hysteria threatened to rise in her throat on a wild laugh.

'Aren't you going to ask me "what conditions"?' His tone was amused, patient, she thought miserably, as if he were humouring the child he must still think her.

'All right!' She lifted her chin proudly. 'What conditions?' For her grandmother's sake, she would have to accept, even at the risk of her own heartache.

'Only one really,' was his cheerful answer, 'that *you* marry me.'

CHAPTER EIGHT

'WHAT a strange idea for a honeymoon!'

That comment had been made by several people and Shari had been forced to smile brightly and respond 'not at all', when in fact she couldn't care less. It was all one to her how they spent these next few dreadful days.

'Well, at least you won't need a trousseau!' had been another favourite among the jesting remarks made at the reception. That was true. Griff had once said that clothes didn't matter. Well, obviously it didn't matter much to him *what* she looked like. He'd got what he wanted, Threlkeld, but *she* was the one paying the price. If she didn't feel so miserable, she could have laughed, at the remembrance of how much she had wanted to marry Griff, but under very different circumstances.

It was late afternoon when they set out, leaving the reception still in full swing. The acrid scent of garden bonfires in their nostrils and the bracken fronds on the fellside just beginning the transformation from uniform green to copper-gold were reminders that summer was nearly over.

'All right?' Griff looked down at Shari, shifting the weight of his haversack slightly, as he spoke.

She didn't answer. Of course she wasn't 'all right'. Everything was all wrong; and to add to her woes, she had to force herself to make the physical exertion necessary for a climbing holiday. It was his idea that they should spend their honeymoon so. Head down, concentrating on placing her feet, she followed her new husband up the mountainside. It wasn't long before the going became rough, a wet, greasy gully, its holds masked with green moss and slime, so that they had to claw and haul their way upwards, Shari disdaining all his offers of help. No wonder he hadn't married Estelle, Shari thought grimly, if this was his notion of a romantic honeymoon. But then, things would have been very different if he'd married the other woman. Then he would have wanted all the real romantic trappings. Estelle warranted them, *she* didn't. He hadn't married her for love.

'But, but you're going to marry Estelle!' had been her first reaction when she'd recovered from the shock of hearing Griff's stipulation.

'No, I'm not,' he contradicted and her heart gave a funny little skip. He sounded quite positive.

'But why on earth do you want to marry me?'

'Have you no idea at all?' he returned gravely.

Dumbly, she shook her head. She hadn't.

'Come here,' he murmured. 'Perhaps this will help you to find the answer.'

She wasn't quite sure if she'd obeyed him, or whether he had pulled her into his arms; but she was there, her head cradled against his shoulder, fitting into the curve of his neck as naturally as if it belonged there and longing stirred within her. Experimentally, she rubbed the side of her head along his jawline, in a gesture that a sensuously content cat might have used. Indeed, she felt that if she *had* been a cat, she would have been purring.

Strong, caressive fingers plunged into the depths of her thick, dark hair, holding it away from her neck so that Griff's lips, as they had done once before, could smooth a trail of kisses from collarbone to ear, her soft lobe a target for his teeth. She gave a little gasp, turning instinctively towards him. Wonderingly, she put up her hand to touch his cheek, found it a little rough beneath her palm, the sensation tinglingly sensuous. She felt him stir and for a disappointed moment, thought he was going to release her; but it had only been to snap off the

overhead light, so that they were totally submerged in a
warm, intimate darkness, hidden from passing, curious
eyes. His lips repeated their exploration by way of her
tender jawline, until they found her mouth, parted by
now in a breathless desire for his possession.

'I remember the first time I kissed you,' he murmured
against her lips. 'You were so sweet, so innocent, and
you're still an innocent, aren't you, Shari?' His grasp
tightened, so that the pleasure was almost painful.
'There's so much I could teach you about love, so much
pleasure I could give you, that we can give each other if
you'll marry me.'

She was trembling uncontrollably now, in an ague of
anticipation. This couldn't be happening to her. It was
too incredibly wonderful, that she should be offered
what she most wanted from life.

Her delicate wrap was brushed aside by a strong,
exploring hand, his touch gentle, but the skin rough
against her smooth shoulders. His lips followed, tracing
a line down over the uncovered expanse of flesh which
had seemed so daring, finding the curve of her breasts
where they emerged from the softly draped bodice, his
tongue delving delicately into the warm, secret cleft
between.

A familiar, dull ache was beginning deep within her,
an aching need she recognised now for what it was, a
need that only he could awaken, only he could satisfy.

'You haven't answered me yet,' he reminded her, his
breath fluttering the delicate material. '*Will* you marry
me?'

In the darkness, in the closeness of his arms, the dear
warmth of his head pressed to her breasts, she was
stifling, floating, burning up in an agony of desire. She
could hardly speak.

'Yes,' she whispered, 'oh yes, please.'

He captured the little hand that had curved shyly
about his neck and held it against his chest.

'Unfasten my shirt,' he urged huskily, 'touch me, Shari, make love to me.'

She had never made love to a man before, but she was learning, fast. One button, then a second yielded to her tremulous, inexperienced fingers. First her hand and then, more daringly, her lips, touched the rough maleness of his chest. Yet another button was undone and she was able to slide both hands inside his shirt, pressing her palms to the hard muscularity of him, sliding round to his smooth back, tracing the line of his spine, downwards, pausing lingeringly at its base.

He gasped and she felt his body tighten in response to her diffident touch. His own hands were working on the zip fastener at the back of her dress and she felt it give readily to his deft persuasion. Released from its only support, the silky material slid down to her waist. Too late she remembered that it had been impossible to wear a bra beneath the dainty bodice, too late she tried to retreat. But her hands were still trapped inside his shirt and his had already taken possession of her small tip-tilted breasts, shaping them as a connoisseur might handle precious porcelain.

'You're beautiful!' His mouth formed the words against the rosy tips that hardened to him. Could he really find her body beautiful compared to Estelle's more generous endowment? It seemed so, for intuitively she sensed a growing urgency in him, could no longer doubt that he was stirred by her. A thrill that was half terror ran through her. Matters were moving a little too fast. She was far too aware of her own ignorance of how to please him, knew that she wasn't ready yet.

'Griff, please, don't, I ...' She choked on her emotion. 'I don't think I can bear any more, without ... I want ...' What did she want? Though her brain could not seem to make sense of the words, her body knew their shape and form and she was flooded with shame, knowing what she wanted him to do, to teach her, now, knowing that he mustn't, that they *must* wait.

His firm, warm lips had reached her waist, the gentle, almost non-existent curve of her flat, boyish stomach; his tongue probed her navel in erotic mimicry of the intimacy he desired. She sensed that very soon it would be too late to cry stop. She shuddered, wanting him to continue, not wanting him to. For a while she tried closing her ears to conscience. If he intended to marry her, did it really matter where and when he first made love to her? Marry her!

A picture swam before her eyes, a photograph her grandmother kept always by her, a picture with which Shari had been familiar since she could toddle, since she could ask questions, a photograph of her grandparents on their wedding-day. Abigail still had the dress, carefully preserved in layers of tissue, old-fashioned in style, but still very, very beautiful.

'I want *you* to wear it some day, Shari, to be a beautiful bride, in white, as I was, a symbol that I was giving myself to my husband, a pure gift, untouched.'

The white of that dress had aged now to palest ivory, but its symbolism remained the same and Shari wanted to wear it, as her grandmother had dreamt she would, wanted to wear it as a bride who proudly acknowledged her right to all it represented, the outward sign of virginity, of her belief in the sanctity of married love. She wanted to give herself to Griff, oh how much she wanted that, but she had absorbed her grandmother's ideals and she wanted to offer him perfection.

With a sudden access of strength that was mental as well as physical, she freed her lips from the passionate possession that threatened to destroy all sense, all willpower.

'Griff, no,' she protested, 'no please, not here. Not like this. If you want me to marry you, I will, but ...' She knew he wasn't hearing her, his mind deafened as

hers had almost been by the growing urges of his body.
She began to use her hands then, not to caress, but to
push, to thrust him away from her. 'Griff!' The protest
came strongly. 'I won't be seduced like this, not in a car. I
don't want it to be that way. It would spoil everything.'

At last she had reached him, her desperate plea
bringing him to his senses. With a muttered expletive of
self-condemnation, he released her and in one violent
movement of his long body he was out of the vehicle,
striding away from it with long, powerful strides, as
though he never meant to return. But she knew he
would. She knew he needed the night air to cool his
fever, the exercise to bring his body under control. She
only wished she could find similar release in action, but
she couldn't get out of the car looking like this and
struggle as she might, she couldn't manage the zip of her
dress. Every part of her body that Griff had touched with
his hands and lips tingled with pangs of unassuaged
desire, cried out for the return of that touch.

He came back to find her half sobbing with
frustration as she fought fruitlessly for self-control,
fought the recalcitrant zip. Immediately he was all
tenderness, his touch comforting now, impersonal
almost, as he helped her straighten her clothing, as he
took her into his arms, cradling her comfortingly.

'It's all right, Shari! It's all right. I'm sorry, love. For
a while there I forgot everything, how young, how
inexperienced you are, everything except how much I
wanted you.'

As she grew calmer, she was able to speak.

'I wasn't rejecting you, Griff. I didn't mean to be
hurtful. It's just that I want to go about things the right
way.' She was able to explain about her grandmother,
about the dress, how she wanted to be able to face
Abigail, to enjoy the pride in her face at the sight of her
granddaughter coming down the aisle, wearing 'the
dress'. 'I want us to have . . . to have mutual respect.'

He listened gravely, understandingly, until at length he released her and started the car.

'It seems it's time I took you home. It's a long way past midnight, little Cinderella.' He laughed softly, but she was still too tense to respond appropriately to his mood.

Griff parked the car in the stable yard and as they walked hand in hand towards the house, he noticed that Shari was limping.

'Did someone tread on your toes?'

Half ashamed, expecting him to laugh at her, she explained about her ill-fitting shoes.

'Here!' He wasn't laughing, but held out his free hand. 'Take the wretched things off and give them to me. See, they'll slip into my pocket. We'll walk across the lawn, unless,' teasingly, 'you'd rather I carried you.'

'No, thank you.' She would have liked that, but it seemed wiser not to relinquish herself once more into his arms.

The soft grass, the night dew were bliss to her aching feet. But without her shoes she felt very much more conscious of her diminutive build, how very vulnerable she was to the tall man who walked beside her, matching his long stride to hers, their thighs brushing occasionally; not deliberately on his part, she was sure, but just as disturbing to her nerves, still vibrantly alive to him.

Would he kiss her good night? she wondered, as they neared the house. She hoped he would, knew she would be disappointed if he didn't. How long did it take to get married? she wondered with a little shiver of anticipation and how would they bear the waiting, either of them?

In the hallway, where only one dim light burned against their return, he drew her to him.

'When shall we get married, Shari?' he asked. It was almost as though he had read her thoughts, his sapphire eyes burning down into the violet ones raised worshipfully, yet doubtfully to his.

'When ... whenever you like,' she murmured, too shy to admit to him that he couldn't desire an early date more fervently than she.

'As soon as possible then?' he suggested, his grasp tightening, breath quickening, his voice husky, excitingly urgent.

'Yes, oh yes,' she whispered, eyes downcast, unable to meet the sudden flare of passion in his.

He picked her up then, easily lifting her slight form until her tremulous, responsive mouth was on a level with his. His lips crushed hers, kiss after kiss bruising their softness, then, deliberate, exquisite, tantalising pleasure, he let her slide sensuously the full length of him, awakening her to a greater knowledge of his bodily needs, and hers. Her nerves quivered. Would he let her go now? And if he didn't, how could she resist his importunities when he had rekindled that flame that burned so close to the surface of her being? Suddenly she knew she must be strong for both of them. With a little gasp and a jerk of her body, she freed herself, the unexpectedness of her movement taking him unawares. She ran for the stairs. Fear that was compounded of her own needs, her knowledge of her own weakness, her own temptation where he was concerned, lent speed to her feet. She heard him call something after her, but she took no notice, running frantically until she reached her room.

Closing the door behind her, she leant against its heavy timbers, badly in need of their support. Her legs felt weak, almost non-existent, as if she had been ill. But then, as she grew calmer, a sense of exaltation took possession of her and she moved around the room in an ecstatic, dreamy waltz, hands clasped to her breast, which felt it must burst to the excited vibrations of her heart. Griff wanted to *marry* her ... to marry *her*, not

Estelle! Now that she was away from the heady, drugging influence of his arms, his insistent kisses, the magnetic pull of his magnificent body, she could begin to realise the wonder of it, to think about it more sanely, to recall, retell to herself the events of the evening. Like a miser recounting his golden hoard, she dwelt upon Griff's words, the lovemaking that had both excited and frightened her, savouring it more perhaps in retrospect than in its seductively mind-shattering reality.

At last she sank down on the edge of her bed, looking around her. Now she wouldn't have to leave Threlkeld. She could stay, though not here, not in this room, which had been hers since childhood. She felt her face glow warm with the implication of her thoughts. Which room would she and Griff choose for their own?

The thought of sharing a room, let alone a bed, with Griff, was so new, so intimate a conception that her mind could scarcely encompass it, imagine the actuality; yet her body vibrated to the notion, like a violin string plucked by the hand of a master. Being in love, being loved by Griff would be the most wonderful experience of her life; it would be *the* experience that transcended all others. Love? Doubtful all of a sudden, she searched her memory for the word. Had he mentioned it? Now that she tried to remember, she couldn't recall either of them actually using it. She, because she had been too shy; and he? She shook her head impatiently. Of course he must love her. Otherwise why should he ask her to marry him. Nothing else made any sense.

On this thought she began to undress, experiencing surprising difficulty with the zip which had responded so readily to Griff's fingers, she recalled. The whisper of oriental silk fell about her feet and she picked it up, caressing its softness as she laid it almost reverently over a chair. It was a very special dress.

Just inside her door next morning Shari found her

shoes, neatly side by side, a slip of paper tucked into one of them.

'Cinderella only left one slipper behind,' the message read in Griff's characteristically heavy black writing. 'I hadn't the heart to ask to try them on your feet, not when you looked more like the Sleeping Beauty. P.S. Why don't *you* wake up when you're kissed?'

Her cheeks glowed. Griff had come into her room last night. He'd seen her asleep, actually kissed her, and she hadn't known it, she mourned.

Abigail Freeman was breakfasting alone, when her granddaughter went downstairs. Shari's eager eyes had immediately registered the fact that Griff wasn't present and disappointment smote her, even though she had been shy about meeting him again. Last night, in the anonymous dark, it had been easier to say and to do things that in daylight she knew she would blush for. Had Griff seen her grandmother this morning? she wondered. Had he said anything?

'Shari, I've been thinking,' Abigail began, before Shari could find a way to introduce the subject that most concerned her. 'Thinking for quite some time, actually. I feel I haven't really been fair to you. I know it couldn't be helped but ... Well, you must have expected that Threlkeld would always be your home, that it would pass to you when I'm gone.'

Shari tried to interrupt, to tell her grandmother it was all right, that the Hall *would* still be her home, now that she was going to marry Griff, but Abigail was holding up one, frail, white hand.

'You don't know this, of course, but Miss Garner told me a few days ago that she thought she'd found a place which would suit her better. She was very apologetic about letting me down at the last moment; but after the first shock, I found I was rather relieved. I couldn't really like the scheme she had for my old home. Since then I've been making plans. Shari, we have to face it, I'm getting older and I'm not in the best of health, though I hope I have a few more years ahead of me, enough anyway to make my deed of gift to you free of death duties.'

'Deed of gift?' Shari was bewildered.

'Yes, darling. I've decided to make Threlkeld over to you, legally. Oh, I know it's really only a token gesture, that you may still have to sell, though I rather think . . .' She paused, then, 'But at least, in any eventuality the money for the sale would be yours.'

'But Gran . . .'

'No, there's no need to say anything, darling. I certainly don't want thanks and I'm not being a bit morbid, so please don't think that, just practical.' Abigail pushed aside her empty cup and stood up. 'Jimmy's driving me into Kendal this morning. The documents are all ready. They just need my signature. Then Threlkeld's yours to do with exactly as you like. To keep if you can, or if not . . .' She smiled a strangely secretive smile, Shari thought. 'But I'm sure things are all going to work out very satisfactorily.'

'But . . .' At last Shari managed to get a word in. 'If you don't sell, where would you get the money to buy your cottage?' Privately, she was determined that this shouldn't happen anyway. Abigail could stay in her old home when Shari married Griff, but she was curious as to how her grandmother's mind was working.

'Well, I do have *some* savings, dear, and so does Lily. We've talked things over and we've decided to pool our resources and buy the cottage between us.'

'Gran?' It was hard to ask the question, because she was afraid of what the answer might be. 'Does . . . does Griff know about this idea of yours?'

'Oh yes, dear. After all, he is Estelle's friend and her financial adviser. Did you know his firm used to handle her godmother's affairs? So when Estelle inherited she left her affairs in their hands. But I've wandered from the point. I'm not a wealthy woman, far from it, but I did ask him to advise *me*, so he certainly knows what I have in mind, though he did say . . .'

'I see!' Shari said grimly, and she thought she did see. Griff had known for some days that Threlkeld was going to be Shari's. Had he feared that, as its owner, she would refuse to sell? No wonder he hadn't mentioned 'love'. Even he hadn't the gall to be that hypocritical. It was Threlkeld that he desired, not her. She was just the key to possession.

So her bitter reflections ran as they climbed ever higher. Under normal circumstances, Shari would have been enjoying this autumn evening. The crag they had reached at last now caught the full glare of the evening sun, surprisingly warm for the time of year. It seemed that, after a late start to the good weather, Lakeland was to have an Indian summer.

Far below them, farmworkers were finishing for the day; they had been getting in the late hay. Cars and coaches, like toy miniatures, were moving slowly homeward with their burden of tired day-trippers. But up here there was no other sound, no other movement, than that of sheep nosing in the bracken.

Griff sat down. He seemed totally relaxed, his eyes appreciatively on the panorama around them. After a while and ostentatiously leaving a gap between them, Shari did the same. He turned then and looked at her. She could feel that appraising sapphire gaze on her stony profile, but she refused to meet his eyes.

'Still don't trust me, do you? Or believe me?' His tone was ruefully amused but it held exasperation too—and hurt? Why should he be hurt just because she had found him out?

Stubbornly she shook her head, her own eyes still fixed determined on the outline of the hills, as sharp as a cardboard cut-out against the blue sky.

'You know, you're going to be sorry about that, soon,' he said, his tone not angry, but holding an annoying certainty.

'Sorry!' she snapped. 'I'm regretting the whole mess already. You know very well I wouldn't have married you if you hadn't forced me into it, blackmailed me.'

'I don't believe you, Shari. That night, after the dance, you were willing enough. You wanted me as I wanted you, only we agreed that we'd wait, so that you and your grandmother could have the sort of wedding you'd always planned.'

'That would sound very noble if I didn't know what a small sacrifice you were making, that you could afford to wait. Couldn't you?' she demanded bitterly. 'Since all you ever really wanted was Threlkeld, so much so that you even talked Estelle out of buying it.'

'Well, at least that should have proved one thing to you,' he said sharply, suddenly retaliating, 'that your stupid jealousy of her was unfounded.'

'Jealous? Me? Of Estelle?' She forced a laugh. 'As far as I was concerned, she was welcome to you, still is.' Her voice broke on what sounded suspiciously like a sob.

'I wonder if you'll still think *that* in a week's time, even in twenty-four hours' time?' As he stood up, apparently ready to continue their climb, she looked at him incredulously. What difference did he think a few days, a few hours were going to make? She'd made it clear enough to him that their bargain didn't include consummating this marriage. As she fell into step behind him once more she remembered that morning, three weeks ago, when she'd had confirmation that Griff had known Threlkeld was to be hers.

She'd seen Abigail off on her trip to Kendal, knowing that it was no good trying to dissuade her grandmother from her plan of making over house and farm to her.

She had long been aware from whom she inherited her own stubborn traits.

With Abigail's departure she'd gone in search of Griff, determined to have out with him the perfidy she suspected and in the process she had, unintentionally, discovered further unpleasant facts to add to her litany of accusations against him. She'd finally tracked him down to Jimmy's office, the sound of his rich, full-bodied laughter that once would have stirred her heart, drifting through the open window, Estelle's higher-pitched amusement providing a descant to his mirth.

'You rat! Griff Masterson! To think you could be so devious! All the years we've been friends and now you tell me you've been angling all along to get Threlkeld for yourself. You could just have *told* me, instead of taking quite such drastic measures.'

Amusement still sounding in his voice, Griff's persuasive reply carried just as clearly to Shari's ears.

'But like all women, my dear, you are incredibly stubborn. Even though *I'm* supposed to be your adviser, if I'd told you Threlkeld wasn't right for you, you'd have gone ahead and bought, told me to get lost and damned the consequences. I had to let you find out for yourself. But you'll forgive me, won't you?' His voice was coaxingly affectionate, a painful sound to the unseen listener. 'After all, you have come out of it better off in the end. The Old Grange is much more suitable for what you have in mind. And think of the mutual advantages we can offer each other. So we're both satisfied? Yes?'

Though despising herself for eavesdropping, Shari lingered nevertheless, out of range of the window, listening intentionally now. She heard the sound of a quick kiss and pain tore through her.

'You know damn well I'd forgive you anything, you unscrupulous old rogue. But I still think you needn't have gone to quite such lengths.'

What lengths? Shari thought she knew. Griff had steered Estelle in the direction of a different property, knowing full well that Threlkeld was to be Shari's and so he had decided to offer marriage. She would sooner have had his money than his insincerity.

There seemed to be no more worth overhearing and so Shari flung open the office door, walking into what appeared to be a cosily intimate scene, Griff in Jimmy's chair with Estelle perched upon its arm, her head close to his as they pored over some documents.

At Shari's abrupt entry, Griff looked up and at once his rugged features broke into the wide smile with its endearing gap in the white teeth, the smile that could make her legs melt beneath her. But not this time, the hypocrite.

'Did you sleep well?'

'I just thought you'd like to know, and your girlfriend too, as she happens to be so handily present, that I take back everything I said last night. I wouldn't marry you if ... if the rest of the male population was composed of hairy apes, and you needn't think I'll sell Threlkeld to you either. I'll let the house fall down round my ears first.'

For a moment or two, her impassioned outburst didn't seem to register, then Griff's jaw hardened and with a significant glance at Estelle, he said quietly, 'Shari, I don't know what's got into you all of a sudden, but I think we'll discuss this somewhere else, if you don't mind. Unless, Estelle, would you excuse us?'

'Oh don't mind me!' Hastily Estelle stood up. 'I'm just off anyway. I promised to look in on Charlie and Elsie now my business affairs are more or less in order.'

'Don't rush off on my account,' Shari said bitterly and to Griff, 'I've nothing I want to discuss with you.' She turned to leave, but her exit was prevented by Estelle's own hurried escape from a situation that promised to become embarrassing, Their collision resulted in time for Griff to round the desk and grasp Shari firmly by the shoulders, marching her back to the centre of the office.

In anger or tenderness, his touch had power to stir her and so she snapped at him.

'Take your hands off me!'

'I will, if you promise to stay right here of your own accord!' His expression was grim and she knew she wasn't going to be allowed to get away without giving him a full explanation, chapter and verse, of her *volte-face*.

'I'm not promising you anything,' she retorted.

'Then I'll just have to keep you here by force.' He suited action to words, pushing her over to the chair he had just vacated, dumping her in it. 'Now!' Grimly, 'What was that little tirade all about?'

'As if you couldn't guess! You and your machinations!' She was glaring at him, but the brilliance of her violet eyes was not all due to rage. Tears lurked there too. Why, oh why had this man, the man she'd believed she idolised, turned out to be a mercenary, underhand?

'Oh, for heaven's sake say what you've come to say, don't beat about the bush, or I might be tempted to beat you!' He leant back against the desk, long legs straddled, hands thrust deeply into his pockets, as though indeed he sought to prevent himself from using them in anger. The gesture strained the material of his trousers across strong, muscular thighs, thighs whose warmth and strength she had known, and Shari, her eyes on a level with this disturbing sight, averted her gaze, biting on her full bottom lip to control its nervous quivering.

'Why can't women be direct and straightforward, like men?' Griff demanded as the silence deepened, threatened to become never ending.

'Direct! Straightforward! Huh!' This hypocrisy suc-

ceeded in goading her into speech. '*You*?
Straightforward? I've seen through you at last and just
in time, thank goodness, to stop me making a
disastrous mistake.'

'And just what is that supposed to mean?' The
restless shifting of his body was ominous.

'It means that I've found out how you planned all
along to get Threlkeld for yourself.' She waited for him
to dare to deny it.

'So! Been eavesdropping, have you?' The words were
calmly spoken, a further goad to her anger.

'Yes, I have. Though I didn't mean to, not at first,
but now I'm glad I did. To think it was *Estelle* I
disliked, resented. Well, at least she didn't try to smarm
round me the way you did, in the most despicable way
there is.' She couldn't help it, she was fast losing control
and the next words came out on an ill-disguised sob.
'Using the fact that you were a man. Oh I was so happy
until you came here, happy and . . .'

'. . . and very innocent?'

'I was certainly innocent of the fact that men like you
existed, unscrupulous men. You couldn't leave me
alone, could you? You made me . . . made me . . . Oh!'
as his hands shot out and jerked her to her feet against
him.

'Made you love me?'

'No!' Struggling fiercely. 'I hate you! I wish I'd
never . . .'

'Promised to marry me?' His grasp was firm, the
strength of his body so familiarly dear. If only she could
trust him again, lean on his strength. If only she didn't
have to fight her love for him, love that wouldn't seem
to die in spite of what she now knew.

'Never met you, that's what I was going to say. And
that promise, about marriage, it's one I don't have to
keep, won't keep.'

'Won't you?' He seemed irritatingly unperturbed. 'So

what do you propose to tell your grandmother in that case?'

'Nothing! She doesn't need to know anything. She doesn't know I . . . we . . .' Held close to him like this it was hard to think coherently, to feed her anger.

'Oh, but she does know, because I told her.'

'Then *I'll* tell her just what you're really like, what you've done, and why.'

'I don't think you'll do anything of the sort,' he said softly, 'because I intend to persuade you otherwise. Besides, just consider her feelings for a moment, instead of your own. Threlkeld is her home.'

'Yes, but after today, legally as *you* very well know, it's mine! You did know that, didn't you? And so you thought you could get it without parting with a penny. If you could just . . .'

'What do you mean, legally, yours? She hasn't? Damn it! I *told* her that wasn't necessary.'

Shari stared up at him coldly.

'I don't know what you're talking about, but it doesn't really matter. What I can't understand is how Estelle . . .'

'My plans were never dependent upon Estelle,' was his surprising interruption.

'Oh?' disbelievingly. 'I thought she was the one with the money?'

'Money?' To Shari his smile seemed infuriatingly patronising. 'You mean her legacy? My dear child, my firm could buy and sell Estelle a thousand times over and not feel the draught.'

'Don't call me a child! Or yours.'

'Why not? Since you're so intent on behaving like one, jumping to unwarranted conclusions, and you *are* going to be mine, make no mistake about that.' It was said fiercely with a hardening of his body against her that made her quiver responsively, despising herself for doing so. 'Anyway, as I was about to say, as well as my being an old friend, my firm also handles Estelle's investments and I decided Threlkeld wasn't the right one for *her*.'

'And yet you let her submit a planning application, hang around waiting for a result? Then there's the appeal.'

'At that time I didn't know what I know now,' he said obscurely. 'But as it turned out, that time proved very useful. I suppose you could say I fell in love ... with Threlkeld. I got to like the locality and the people. I matured my own plans.'

'So you do have one virtue then!' she said acidly. 'Patience!'

'More than you know!' he said with significance. 'And you don't really know me, do you, Shari? Not even after all this time.'

'No thank goodness, and I don't have to get to know you any better. Because I don't want to. Can't you understand? I despise you, your underhand methods, pretending you wanted to marry me, letting me take the blame for ...'

'I let you take the blame for nothing!' he said sternly. 'I even told Estelle you hadn't signed that petition, that you hadn't instigated it.'

'How could you possibly be sure of that?' Then, defiantly, 'I might have done!'

'How?' He smiled. 'When Jimmy confessed that he'd signed on your behalf? Actually, I found the whole thing very amusing. You see *I* was responsible for starting that petition.'

'Here we are then! the honeymoon suite!' Griff's deliberately light-hearted words penetrated the fog of unhappy reminiscence that had occupied Shari for the last thousand or so feet.

She looked around her, recognising her surroundings for the first time; recognised the little hut, typical of many located on the high fells, but much higher up than most of them. Few climbers ever passed this way.

Originally the hut had been the ruined shell of a quarry building, but the quarry had been deserted for years and the hut had been rebuilt, secured against the weather. Shari had slept there many times before, though not of recent years, accompanied by Charlie Garner, her father and Jimmy. In childhood she had revelled in these weekends spent away from the more civilised comforts of home, had thrilled to simple pleasures such as that of waking at dawn to watch the sun flooding the valleys far below. After a day's hard climbing its elementary comforts of shelter, food and warmth had been as welcome as that of a four-star hotel.

How had Griff learned of this place? she wondered. He hadn't revealed their destination and now, she reflected bitterly, these next few days were going to ruin for her something that still held nostalgically re-membered pleasures, the memories of her untroubled, carefree youth.

This hut, by virtue of its remoteness, was one of the smaller of its kind, its rather crude quarters housing only four people at any one time. There were no sleeping-bunks. They had always used sleeping-bags or cocoons of blankets, cushioned by piles of dry, fragrant bracken. In winter, an old-fashioned stove, stoked up at bedtime, had kept them reasonably warm until morning. It had been fun, that sense of pioneering, but Shari did not expect any pleasure from this present expedition.

It would have been so different, she thought wistfully, if she had been happily, ecstatically in love. Then this plain little oblong box of a building with its single window, its inconveniences, could have been a haven.

They would have laughed, she and Griff, over the primitive facilities, made an adventure of its drawbacks, lost to all other needs but that of their desire for each other.

She still loved Griff. Painfully, she conceded to herself that this was a burden from which her heart could never be free. But there was no winged ecstasy in this love, only a heavy, suffocating sensation in her throat, a dragging hopelessness of spirit that deadened her senses to the Lakeland beauties surrounding her, and all because he didn't love her, just the possession that was hers, Threlkeld.

While she stood, brooding, at the entrance to the hut, Griff had been busily unpacking the contents of his rucksack, transferring them to the simple storage space the hut afforded, lighting the ancient stove.

'Shari!'

Unwillingly, she responded to the command in his voice and moved inside, removing her own rucksack, sinking down despondently on to the wooden bench that ran along two walls of the hut and watching him.

'How about a drink?'

Dumbly, she nodded. She supposed she should be the one attending to their creature comforts, but somehow, suddenly, everything had caught up with her: the long climb, the problems that had beset her over the past weeks, especially the mounting tensions as her wedding-day had approached, her apprehensions regarding the next few hours, days, the rest of her life! For it never even entered Shari's head to consider that one day, divorce might be a means of escape. She believed in the sanctity of the vows she had taken, even though she had been forced by circumstances to do so. Fatigue dragged at her limbs, her reactions, and the slender hands she held out for the warm drink trembled.

Griff squatted before her, his rugged features concerned, his hands steadying hers, guiding the mug to her lips. The contact sent a current of unwilling awareness along her nerves. They were up here, just the two of them, quite alone, miles from any other human agency and she was so vulnerable to her need of him; a need which because of his despicable behaviour it was necessary to fight, to deny.

Briefly her eyelids fluttered up, her gaze meeting Griff's steady sapphire regard and she felt the familiar longing for him wash over her. Her pulses jumped disturbingly and breathing seemed even more difficult than it had during their climb. Disconcerted, she spoke what was in her mind.

'Why?' She whispered the words despairingly, more revealingly than she knew. 'Why did you have to make me hate you?'

He took away the now empty mug, but his hands returned to hold hers.

'Are you sure that you do?' His voice was gentle, its seeming tenderness almost her undoing; but he was a consummate actor, she must remember that, and she fought back the fatigue-induced moisture of emotion that darkened her eyes, her head nodding wordlessly.

'Right now you may think you do,' he said, 'but you're all mixed up, Shari. You don't really understand everything. And since you've avoided me these past few weeks, I haven't had a chance to answer your accusations.'

'To tell me more lies,' she said. There was no acrimony in her tone, only a dreadful weariness of spirit.

'I've never lied to you! Never!' he asserted. No? perhaps he hadn't. After all, he'd never pretended to love her! 'I'll admit I kept certain things from you, but I had very good reasons! Believe me,' he urged. 'Shari, love, won't you let me tell you my side of things? At least hear me out. Then, if I haven't convinced you . . .' He shrugged and she wondered cynically what course of action he proposed to follow in that case. 'At least let's call a truce for an hour or so, hmm?'

'All right,' she said doubtfully, tremulously. It was

only fair to give him a hearing; but if only he knew how little she wanted to fight him.

He looked down thoughtfully at their clasped hands, as if he were deciding just where he should begin his explanations. Please let me be able to believe him, Shari pleaded inwardly. Please let him tell the truth, truth that I know is irrefutable. He turned her hands over and pressed his lips to each palm in turn, the warmth of his lips against the soft flesh sending an electrifying sensation throughout her whole body.

A violent storm of feeling shook her. Every pulse in her body clamoured for a repetition of that kiss; her mouth ached for him to kiss her on the lips. She stared at him, violet eyes darkened to pansy-brown with emotion.

'It's been a long day for you,' he said. 'You look fagged out. Why don't you get ready for bed? We can talk just as easily there.'

The thought of rest for her weary body was irresistible and she nodded, agreeable to his suggestion, until he pulled her to her feet and she saw where he was indicating that she should rest! in a *double* sleeping-bag; the other half of which she had no doubt he intended to occupy. When he'd said he would carry most of the equipment she'd had no doubt that his pack contained two single bags. It hadn't occurred to her for one moment, especially in view of what she'd said, made quite clear to him.

'No, I can't . . . we're not . . .' She shuddered at the images that filled her brain, erotic images that tensed her stomach muscles in an attempt to fight the sudden storm of mixed emotions, desire and revulsion.

'Why not?' He sounded amused. 'After all, we *are* married.'

'I know, but I told you I wouldn't . . . and besides. I don't know yet that I *will* believe what you say. So you needn't think you're going to convince me by . . .'

'By making love to you?' Soft-voiced, he stated the
fear she could not. 'Suppose I promise I won't lay so
much as a finger on you unless and until *you* ask me to?
Until you tell me something I haven't heard you say,
that you love me?'

She ask him? How could she be the one to initiate
such a move? Even if he convinced her a hundred times
over, she would be too shy; and why should she admit
her love when he had never even pretended to feel that
emotion for her? Desire he *had* admitted to, but nothing
more.

'I think I'd rather stay here for the moment.' She
retreated to the uncomfortable wooden bench.

'Look, Shari!' For the first time he showed signs of
impatience with her. 'It's autumn and the nights get
cold anyway, but up here we're at nearly three thousand
feet. Soon you're going to *need* some extra warmth.'

Stubbornly she shook her head. She couldn't get into
that sleeping bag with him, she just couldn't. However
much he promised not to touch her, contact of some
kind was almost inevitable, as would be her undoing. In
such proximity it would be impossible to hide her
reactions to him. She wasn't relaxing her determination
by one iota. Even if he could convince her that he was
innocent of the charges she'd laid against him, she
wasn't going to weakly admit her love for him.

Griff shrugged his shoulders.

'O.K. But you'll soon change your mind when I put
the lamp out and you start to get cold.'

No physical coldness, she told herself, could be worse
than the numbness of spirit she had felt these last
weeks, and she remained silent, averting her eyes as he
undressed and slid into the sleeping-bag. The lamp was
extinguished; there was a long silence.

Griff had been right, damn him. The hut *was* growing
steadily colder and with the chill came a deepening of
her depression.

'I thought you wanted to talk,' she said, a touch of desperation in her voice. How could he sleep, when she needed him to explain away her doubts?

'Yes, when you decide to be sensible.' His answer came swiftly, alertly. So he hadn't fallen asleep as she'd feared. Then, his voice warmly coaxing, 'Come to bed, Shari, love. It will all sort itself out, I promise you . . .'

To her horror, at the kindness in his voice she felt tears prick her eyes, begin to run down her cold cheeks. Unwarily, she sniffed and Griff stirred restlessly.

'You're crying!'

'N . . . no . . .' she sobbed.

'You're cold! *Aren't you?*'

She hadn't intended to answer, to admit it, but another involuntary sob of misery escaped her.

'Yes!'

'Then come here, damn you! And get into this bag, or I'll come and make you.'

She was too cold to resist any more, too unhappy. Perhaps warmth would soothe her to sleep, so that for a few hours, she could forget her woes. Swiftly she undressed, then, carefully, slid in beside him, trying not to touch him. But she needn't have worried. He seemed to have withdrawn to the furthest limits their sleeping accommodation would allow. She lay very still on her back, trying to control her nervous trembling.

'Better?' he asked.

She dared not reply. She knew her tone would be too full of misery still, full of her weak longing to be loved, to have all her doubts and fears caressed away. But her silence was fatal. One strong, calloused hand touched her bare shoulder and it was no longer possible to conceal her uncontrollable shivering. He had promised not to touch her but before she could protest, with a muffled curse, Griff had put his arms about her, pulling her roughly against him. She made a feeble attempt to resist, but the warmth of his body *was* comforting and as he remained still, making no alarming moves, insidiously her tense nerves began to relax. Disturbing though Griff's nearness was, cold and fatigue were now greater than her physical awareness and Shari slept.

It was barely light when she woke. In the night, still clasped in his arms, she had turned towards Griff and now his face was close to hers, his breath a steady, warm flow against her cheek. In the dimness she was just able to discern the strong features, relaxed in sleep. Why had he let her fall asleep, when he had still not stated his case? He must have known how easy it would have been, in her weakened state, to use his physical powers to move her; yet he hadn't even attempted to make love to her. Unwilling respect, admiration moved within her. Had he meant what he said then? That it would be up to *her* to make the first move? Certainly, right now, she felt an irresistible desire to trace his features with her fingers. Would they ever be as close as this again, after they'd talked?

An unwary sigh of longing escaped her and his eyes snapped open. Taken by surprise, she found herself gazing into the sleepy sapphire depths. For a moment he seemed bemused, then a smile parted his lips, he yawned and stretched, a movement which brought his entire body into contact with hers and with a sense of shock, she realised he was entirely naked, something which had never occurred to her. For her own part she had slept in bra and panties, scant protection though they might offer. It would never have occurred to her to sleep in the nude.

'Sleep well?' he asked and she nodded, lowering her eyes, conscious of the blush her discovery had induced. Her throat constricted and she swallowed, as she fought her body's urge to press closer to him, to feel that delicious muscular hardness once more. She thought she sensed a gathering tension in him too, but then he said abruptly, 'Feel more like talking now?'

'I wanted to talk last night,' she said sharply, her nerves unbearably irritated by frustration.

'You were too tired, not thinking clearly. You haven't been thinking clearly for weeks.'

'That's for *you* to prove!' she retorted.

'Shari!' There was a husky edge to his voice. 'Why do you think I persuaded Estelle not to buy your home, why do you think I intended to buy it myself?'

'That's obvious,' she said scornfully. 'Because you wanted it for yourself.'

'No!' He put up a hand and touched the tangled disorder of her silky dark hair. 'I wanted to buy it so that I could give it back to you, so that I could have both of you, you *and* Threlkeld.'

'I don't believe you,' she whispered. 'You *had* to marry me to *get* Threlkeld. Remember, I heard you and Estelle talking about it. You were laughing about how owning two places could be to your advantage, yours and hers, and ...' A small hiccuping sob escaped. '*She* said you needn't have gone to such lengths to get what you wanted, meaning that you needn't have proposed to me.'

'Meaning,' he contradicted, 'that I needn't have organised that petition, and if you heard that, you must have heard me tell Estelle that it would have been no good my taking the direct approach with her. I had to let her find out for herself that Threlkeld wasn't for her before I told her that I wanted it, and why.'

'But my grandmother ruined all your plans, didn't she?' Shari persisted. 'If she hadn't decided to make over Threlkeld to me, you could have bought it, you wouldn't have had to marry me to get it. Then you and Estelle could have had ...'

'Shari!' His voice was stern and he jerked her closer, the sudden contact making her gasp. 'Let's get this

straight, once and for all. It was you I wanted to marry.
I've never had any intention of marrying Estelle, not
ever, or she of marrying me. God damn it! We've
known each other all our lives. It would have been like,'
he sought for imagery, 'like marrying my own sister, no
excitement, no adventure. Then,' he breathed, with a
sinuous, suggestive move of his body against hers,
'there would have been no thrill, the kind I feel when I
do this . . . and this . . .'

'No, Griff, don't.'

'Come here, damn you!' His mouth took hers by
storm, his kiss probing her resistance, making her limp
with longing. It became a fierce passionate exploration
as she gave up the attempt to fight him off and she was
spinning, drifting on a hot, engulfing tide that would
soon, if she were not careful, swamp even common
sense.

But her heart was thudding in rapturous union with
the beat of his own. Strong thighs strained against her.
He needed her and she, oh God, how could she bear
this sensual provocation he was urging upon her?

But it seemed he was still in control, even though she
was fast losing the fight to hide her need to respond, for
he was speaking again.

'Your grandmother asked my advice about making
the house over to you. I advised against it.'

'Of course you would!' she said indignantly, her
fevered longing cooling. 'And it's obvious why.'

'No, it's not. I have my pride, Shari. I didn't *want*
you to make the very mistake you have made, thinking
that I'd married you for Threlkeld, and it *is* a mistake,
because in fact Threlkeld *isn't* yours.'

'Isn't? What do you mean? That isn't true! My
grandmother . . .'

'No! After you'd told me just what you thought of
me and swept out of the office, I got on the telephone
to Kendal. I was just in time to speak to Mrs Freeman

before she signed those papers, and I was able to persuade her to change her mind. I told her Threlkeld would be your home anyway, and hers too, when you married me. After a while, knowing you and your impetuous nature, she saw the point of my argument. Threlkeld is mine, to do with as I please.'

'Oh!' Angrily, she beat small fists against the hardness of his chest. 'You're ... you're despicable, going behind my back like that, turning my own grandmother against me, stealing my home. Well, I hope all your beastly plans fall through. I hope they turn down that appeal. Then perhaps you'll wish you hadn't been so clever. You'll be stuck with just an old, run-down farm, and me ...'

He didn't answer, but freed one hand to reach out for his rucksack, lying not far away. From one of the unbuckled flaps, he drew out a sheet of paper and handed it to Shari.

'This came the day before yesterday,' he told her, 'it's my wedding present to you.' He watched her expressive little face as she read, disbelievingly, the official letter which upheld the appeal, gave permission for Threlkeld's conversion to commercial purposes, and he had dared, sneeringly, to call *this* her wedding present.

'I see!' Her tone was bitter as she threw down the paper and turned her head away, so that he shouldn't see the glitter of tears in her eyes. From now on she would betray no weaknesses of any sort to him.

'No, you don't, not quite. But you will.' He forced the paper back into her unwilling hand. 'Go on, take it, tear it up!'

Her head snapped back towards him, violet eyes bright with unshed tears, wide with surprise.

'Go on! Do it!'

One more doubtful look at him, still uncertain that at the last moment, he would not snatch the paper back, that this was not some further malicious jest at her expense, she shredded the document into tiny pieces. Then she looked at him again, eyes dark with bewilderment.

'Why?' she asked simply.

'Because I want to keep Threlkeld as it is, as I've come to love it, as you love it. I want to be a farmer, get away from city life. I want to follow up my idea for breeding ponies. And *that's* where Estelle and I can be of benefit to each other. I'll hire her the ponies for her holiday-makers and with her larger acres, she can provide me with hay.'

'I see.' He had it all worked out. 'So where do I come into this cosy arrangement? It doesn't seem as if you need me at all.'

'You think not?' He pressed closer to her, his hands moving up slowly, gently, to caress her breasts; and these she could not prevent from responding treacherously to his persuasion.

'Why did you threaten me?' she asked, desperately trying to distract her attention, which now seemed centred on the movement of his hands, attending competently to the removal of her bra. 'Why did you blackmail me into marrying you, by saying my grandmother could only stay in her home if I ...'

'Would you have married me otherwise? In the mood you were in?'

'No.'

'Shari, I wanted *you* beside me, working that farm, helping me to realise my ambitions, giving me sons to inherit what I intend to make of Threlkeld.' He paused, his hand moving lower, down over her hips, seeking warm, soft places that leapt into life at his touch, and though her brain might still doubt, her body was all too ready to be convinced. 'Loving me,' he continued, his voice ragged, as though the words were difficult of utterance.

'Why *me*?' But she was beginning to suspect ... glorious suspicion ... if only he would confirm it.

'That's for *you* to tell *me*?' Subtly, his movements were becoming faster, increasingly urgent, his emotions running high, and yet he was still in control.

But Shari was trembling as violently as if he were in fact taking possession of her. She could feel the tremors in the limbs pressed to hers, recognise his undoubted need. Their bodies were crying out for fulfilment, why deny them any longer? And yet there was more to this need than physical assuagement. She couldn't yet bring herself to make that final, verbal commitment; but she could ask, a nervous, tentative question.

'Is it ... is it because you love me? You've never actually said that you ...'

'Nor have you,' he reminded her and she recognised the implacable evasion for what it was. He had said she must take the initiative.

Greatly daring, she let her fingers go on their own voyage of discovery, caressing the satin smoothness of his flesh, feeling the narrowing curve of his waist below the taut ribcage, the flatness of his stomach with its roughening of body hair.

'Is that what you want me to say?' she whispered. 'That I ... I ...'

His seductively moving hands had discovered the destination they sought and a long, muscular leg held her prisoner. It was agony, sweet agony, feeling the pressure of him, his hardness, his throbbing desire. She knew that sensation, for both of them, was reaching that final climax that could only be overcome in one way, and a little sound rose in her throat. Another hairsbreadth of movement and she could be irrevocably his, but he wouldn't make it, until ...

'Do *you want* to say it?' He was inflexible in his demand.

'Yes!' She whispered the word, her lips pressed to his throat, where a restless pulse throbbed jerkily.

'Then say it! Show me! Show me that you believe in me ... trust me.'

She did believe him now, trusted him. His insistence that she destroy that document had quenched the last spark of doubt, and his body was telling her what he refused to say, until *she* had committed *herself*. It was only her natural shyness now, she realised, her own lack of experience, that held her back. Suppose she failed to please him? Disjointed remarks of her grandmother's, spoken over the years, floated back into her bemused mind: 'Love is a two-way thing.' 'You have to meet each other half way.' 'Sometimes one must go more than half way.' 'You must give as well as receive.'

Her doubts vanished. There was no shame, no damage to her pride in being the first to admit her feelings, especially since she had no real doubts now that they *were* reciprocated in full. Just a few simple words stood between her and all that she fervently desired.

She took a deep breath, moving closer to Griff, sliding her arms about him, deliberately pressing closer. She felt the responsive shudder that shook him, felt his lips against her hair, his voice, husky with feeling, murmuring indistinctly. She lifted her face, meeting his eyes, squarely fearlessly.

'I love you!' She said it softly then, emotion flooding her whole being with an ecstatic fervour, 'Oh, I love you, I *love* you.'

Desperate urgency prompted her to invite his kiss. There was a brief flutter of panic as his tongue experimentally outlined her mouth. Then as his kiss deepened, she responded with an ardour of which she had not known herself capable. She recognised that her trembling was arousing him to an even greater desire, just as he was awakening all the untried sensuality of her own nature.

Despite the inexperience which had troubled her, she seemed to know instinctively how to inflame him further. But what about affection? He had made her admit her feelings, but what about his for her? She drew an unsteady breath, dragging her mouth from his, holding him determinedly away from her.

'And *you*, Griff?' she demanded. 'What about you?'

'Shari!' He groaned her name. 'Oh, my darling, can you still really doubt it? I think I've loved you from the moment I first set eyes on your angry, mutinous little face, and when you showed such guts, such determination, I knew you were the one woman for me. But you were so shy, so wild, like an unbroken pony, I was scared. If I spoke too soon you might shy away, and then there was Jimmy. You were always insinuating that Jimmy . . .'

She laid a finger on his lips.

'Jimmy is a good friend, more like a brother than a friend, and as you said about Estelle . . .'

'So.' He drew a deep breath, as though he needed its steadying strength. 'You love me, I love you, but there's more to it than just words, isn't there? Shari, I don't want to rush you. Are you ready for that kind of love? You're not afraid of me?'

Afraid? When she loved him in every way, with mind, heart, soul, body?

'I'm not afraid,' she said simply. How easy it was after all, to use the language of love without embarrassment. 'I love you, I want you, and I want you to teach me how to please you . . .'

His warm, demanding mouth silenced her; increasing urgency tremored their bodies as they gave full rein to their aching need. It seemed they could not be close enough. Floating, spinning, swinging up to dizzy pinnacles, swamping, drowning in depths of desire. The sweetness of the empty void within her brought moisture to her eyes.

'I never realised,' she gasped, 'that love would be like this.'

'Hush, hush, my darling ...' Again his mouth covered hers, as his body covered *her* body, making it one continuous mould with his, rousing her to such intolerable heights of longing that she wished he would let her speak, so that she could beg him for release, to finally make her his.

Then his movements intensified; she felt the sensitive, considerate thrust of his invasion. There was no need for such care, excitement rose, explosive, akin to anguish, mounting, until together they died that little death that is the natural climax of all lovers. Then they rested, languorously satisfied, at peace with themselves, with each other and with the surrounding hills that enfolded and guarded their first moments of rapture.

HARLEQUIN HISTORICAL

Explore love with Harlequin in the Middle Ages, the Renaissance, in the Regency, the Victorian and other eras.

Relive within these books the endless ages of romance, set against authentic historical backgrounds. Two new historical love stories published each month.

HIST-B-1

ATTRACTIVE, SPACE SAVING BOOK RACK

Display your most prized novels on this handsome and sturdy book rack. The hand-rubbed walnut finish will blend into your library decor with quiet elegance, providing a practical organizer for your favorite hard-or soft-covered books.

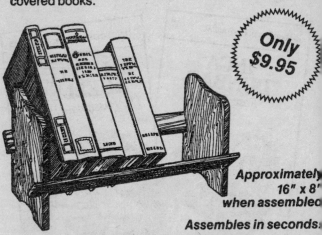

Only $9.95

Approximately 16" x 8" when assembled

Assembles in seconds!

Six exciting series for you every month... from Harlequin

Harlequin Romance·
The series that started it all

Tender, captivating and heartwarming...
love stories that sweep you off to faraway places
and delight you with the magic of love.

◆

Harlequin Presents·

Powerful contemporary love stories...as individual as the women who read them

The No. 1 romance series...
exciting love stories for you, the woman of today...
a rare blend of passion and dramatic realism.

◆

Harlequin Superromance®
It's more than romance...
it's Harlequin Superromance

A sophisticated, contemporary romance-fiction
series, providing you with a longer,
more involving read...a richer mix of complex plots,
realism and adventure.

Harlequin American Romance
Harlequin celebrates the American woman...

...by offering you romance stories written about American women, by American women for American women. This series offers you contemporary romances uniquely North American in flavor and appeal.

◆

Harlequin Temptation
Passionate stories for today's woman

An exciting series of sensual, mature stories of love...dilemmas, choices, resolutions... all contemporary issues dealt with in a true-to-life fashion by some of your favorite authors.

◆

Harlequin Intrigue
Because romance can be quite an adventure

Harlequin Intrigue, an innovative series that blends the romance you expect... with the unexpected. Each story has an added element of intrigue that provides a new twist to the Harlequin tradition of romance excellence.

Harlequin Books

PROD-A-2

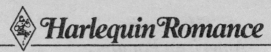# Harlequin Romance

Coming Next Month

2821 ROAD TO LOVE Katherine Arthur
A free-lance photographer happens upon a Clark Gable
look-alike and a chance to pay off her debts. So when he takes
off across America in his shiny silver semi, little does he know
she's along for the ride.

2822 THE FOLLY OF LOVING Catherine George
Times are tough, and it seems foolhardy for an Englishwoman
to turn down a famous actor's marriage proposal. But he broke
her heart eight years ago. So hasn't he done enough already?

2823 WINTER AT WHITECLIFFS Miriam Macgregor
The owner of Whitecliffs sheep station in New Zealand puts
his ward's tutor on a month's trial, and all because he thinks
she's after his half brother. But if he knew where her true
interests lay...

2824 THE SECRET POOL Betty Neels
A nurse's holiday in Holland seems the perfect escape from the
critical appraisal of a certain Dutch doctor—until he tracks her
down, having decided she's perfect for a particular job after all.

2825 RUDE AWAKENING Elizabeth Power
A computer programmer, accused by her suspicious-minded
boss of stealing company secrets, finds herself kept prisoner by
him until she can prove her innocence.

2826 ROUGH DIAMOND Kate Walker
The volatile attraction a young Englishwoman felt for her rebel
from the wrong side of the tracks is reignited years later—along
with the doubts and confusion that drove them apart.

Available in March wherever paperback books are sold, or
through Harlequin Reader Service.

In the U.S.
P.O. Box 1397
Buffalo, N.Y.
14240-1397

In Canada
P.O. Box 603
Fort Erie, Ontario
L2A 5X3

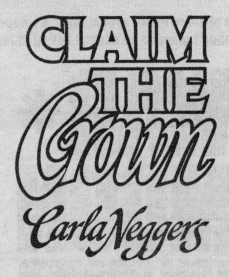